CARMEN BROWNE SERIES #3

Stephanie Perry Moore

MOODY PUBLISHERS
CHICAGO

© 2006 by
STEPHANIE PERRY MOORE

All Scripture quotations are taken from the King James Version.

Cover Design: Lydell Jackson, JaXon Communications
Editor:Tanya Harper

Library of Congress Cataloging-in-Publication Data

Moore, Stephanie Perry.
     Golden spirit / by Stephanie Perry Moore.
        p. cm. — (Carmen Browne series ; bk. #3)
     Summary: Ten-year-old Carmen asks for God's help in
meeting the challenges of her bossy nature and in facing
serious issues such as domestic violence.
     ISBN-13: 978-0-8024-8169-6
     [1. Christian life—Fiction. 2. Friendship—Fiction.
3. Family violence—Fiction. 4. African Americans—Fiction.
5. Virginia—Fiction.] I. Title. II. Series: Moore, Stephanie
Perry. Carmen Browne series ; bk. #3.

PZ7.M788125Go 2006
[Fic]—dc22

                                                      2005029225

ISBN: 0-8024-8169-8
ISBN-13: 978-0-8024-8169-6

3 5 7 9 10 8 6 4

Printed in the United States of America

For Leon
(the foster child we spent time with during the summer of '05)

God blessed me by sending you my way.
Keep letting your golden spirit shine for God.
Always know the Moore family is here for you.
I pray you and every reader remembers you are all special.

Contents

Acknowledgments

I was so tired of refereeing between my girls and their friends. See, Syndi turned nine (where did the years go?), and after an all-girls dance party, Syndi and Sheldyn both chose a girlfriend to spend the night. It should have been fun, but every few minutes someone was whining about not getting her way. Frustrated, I prayed, *Lord, help these four girls learn how to not be so bossy.*

Thankfully, the girls worked it out and their friends actually stayed over another night. I couldn't be too mad because I remembered when I was young, my friends and I struggled over wanting control as well. Now that I'm older, I've learned that to have lasting friendships you have to compromise. I pray every reader learns this important lesson as well. So here's a big thank you to all those who help keep my spirit uplifted so that I can have less stress and write.

To my parents, Dr. Franklin and Shirley Perry, Sr.— you're my role models. I was blessed to have been raised in your stable, safe, loving, two-parent home.

To my Moody Publishers' Lift Every Voice team, especially, the board members—your dedication to this imprint blesses many. I'm so thankful you've gotten behind my writing.

To my daughter's first-grade classmate—so sorry your world was changed because of domestic violence. Know people are praying for you and your siblings.

To my strong-willed, spunky little ladies, Syndi and Sheldyn—you are my inspiration. Keep sharing.

To my Derrick, the man who loves me. So glad we work out our differences God's way.

To my special young readers, this book was written to speak to your soul. I pray through this novel you'll open your heart and let Jesus Christ in.

And to my Heavenly Father, thanks for making my life golden with Your presence. I'm glad I found You at a young age.

1

Dark Hour

My world was so perfect. I was doing well in school. I had two great girl-friends. I even had a boy who liked me. More important than any of that, what made me happy was knowing that my family was happy.

It was Friday night. Two more weeks of school to go. And instead of doing anything with my friends, or doing anything by my-self, we were having family movie night.

My mom and my dad were nestled on the couch together. Dad was thrilled to be head coach of the Virginia State Trojans football team. Soon he would be preparing for what hopefully would be a good year. My mom's art business had really taken off.

She was going to paint murals for all of the Chesterfield County schools. They wanted her to finish twelve of them before the summer was over. Boy, was she really going to be busy.

My brother, Clay, had finally adjusted to the fact that we were his family; adoption didn't matter. He loved us and we loved him, and the problems he was having with my father were gone. My dad wanted him to play football in middle school. Clay wasn't having it at first, but now all of a sudden he had developed an interest. With the good throwing arm he had, I thought he'd be a dynamite quarterback. That made my dad feel good. Even Cassie wasn't bothering me as bad. I realized that my little sister loved me. Over the last couple of weeks we'd been able to talk through our differences. We hadn't been fighting like we normally did.

It was a great night. I had the movie, the popcorn, and all of my family. I could enjoy this scene forever. No sooner than I thought that, the quietness changed.

"Y'all hear that?" my dad asked as he got up from the couch.

Everybody looked at each other sort of confused. I said, "Yeah, Dad, I heard it. That sounds like police sirens or something."

My dad went out the front door and stood on the steps. The rest of us looked out the windows. Two police cars quickly headed toward a house down the street.

"Mom, it looks like they're at Shante's house," Cassie

said in a scared tone. "What's going on over there, Mom? What's going on?"

I couldn't look out the window anymore. Something wasn't right.

"I hope Michael's okay," my brother said, biting his nails, like a person eating corn on the cob.

I didn't know the Thomas family that well. Their son Michael was the middle school bully. He'd picked on me about the way I talked when I first moved to Ettrick, and that hurt my feelings pretty bad. Boy, did I hate running into him on the street. He was so mean. Lately, Cassie had been playing with his sister, Shante. Cassie's best friend was Riana's little sister, but she was starting to hang with Shante too. I thought the Thomas family had some younger children too, but I wasn't sure. Even though I didn't know the family that well, I certainly didn't want anything to be wrong.

"Mom, Shante told me that she was scared, because at night her mom and dad keep fussing. She told me yesterday in school that she never gets to sleep, because they yell all the time. Mommy, what's wrong down there?" Cassie cried as my mom held her.

My dad came back inside the house. "Honey, some of the neighbors and I are going down the street to the Thomases' house. We're going to talk with the police to see what's going on. Y'all stay in the house."

The good movie we were watching didn't matter at that moment. The yummy popcorn was now sitting in a bowl untouched. The perfect silence that we had enjoying each other's company was gone, and our neighborhood was loud, loud, loud. What in the world was going on at ten o'clock at night in the Thomases' house?

About thirty minutes later, my dad came back and he didn't look happy at all. "Guys, I've got some really bad news."

My mother looked as if she was holding her breath. The look on her face frightened me. Part of me didn't want to know what my dad had to share. I only wanted to know good things in life. I didn't want to hear anything bad.

My dad came over and held mine and Cassie's hands as he sat on the couch and said, "Tonight Mr. Thomas made a very bad decision. I don't know all the details, but he and Mrs. Thomas were arguing. He hit her pretty badly. She is unconscious. They rushed her to the hospital. The police took him to jail, and her mother is there with the kids. It's not a good situation. We need to pray for them."

My mom said, "Oh, Charles, no."

My little sister grabbed my dad's arm. She was crying so hard. I felt awful. Mrs. Thomas just had to come around.

My dad led us in prayer. "Lord, right now my family is coming to You because our hearts are broken. We don't understand why bad things happen sometimes, but we trust You to take care of the bad things and make them better. I don't know exactly what happened down the street to cause this, Lord. I mean, my family was down here having a great time enjoying each other, and just a few houses down the street there was a battle going on. We now lift up Mrs. Thomas. We ask that You make her well. We pray for the Thomas kids. Keep them strong as they go through this tough ordeal."

Cassie couldn't stop crying. Seeing her tears and knowing what just happened, I started sobbing too. This was a lot to handle.

My dad continued, "Lord, I pray for Mr. Thomas too. We hope he finds You."

Later in bed, I prayed tomorrow would be a brighter day. The end of this one had taken away my happy spirit and I wanted it back.

✪

When I woke up the next day, I immediately went to my knees. I needed to talk to God. I was so fortunate to have a mom and dad who loved each other. I was thankful that my dad was not violent like Mr. Thomas. Although my mom and dad didn't get along all the time, at least they talked things through. I just wish more adults in the world would do the same thing.

I prayed silently, *Lord, this is tough. I don't understand. Why do adults fight? I'm just asking You to help people talk stuff out more. People shouldn't get so upset at one another.*

Folks should not always have to have their way. And thank
You so much for my mom and dad. Thank You for helping
them love each other so much. I used to say "ugh" when they
kissed, but now I want to see them do that more often. I pray
this prayer in Jesus' name. Amen.

"Carmen, honey, you'd better hurry up and get
dressed," Mom said, interrupting my thoughts. "Mr. Golf
will be here any minute."

With everything that happened the night before, I
had completely forgotten that this was Kings Dominion
Theme Park day. I had planned this a few weeks back,
along with my girlfriends, Layah Golf, who lived with her
dad, and Riana Anderson, who lived down the street with
her dad, mom, and two siblings.

I had been to Kings Dominion several times before
with my family. We had made it a Browne summer family
outing. We didn't get to go last summer, though, because
we moved.

Mother's Day was just around the corner, and Layah
and her dad always did something special around this
time, since her mom moved away. She told Riana and me
that she really didn't care that her mom wasn't living with
them, but it was something about the sadness in her eyes
that told us she wasn't telling the truth. I so wished I
could snap my fingers and make that situation change for
her, but I wasn't God. I couldn't do that, but what I could
do was pray for her and make sure to be a good friend. So
when she asked Riana and me to tag along on the special

16

date with her dad, we were happy to agree. Kings Dominion had the best roller coaster rides, tasty elephant ears, and coolest arcade games in the world.

It took me no time to put on my jeans, T-shirt, and my brand-new, black Nikes. My mom had given me thirty dollars, and since Mr. Golf said he would take care of my entrance fee, I had that money to spend on whatever I wanted. I planned to spend it wisely.

Riana and I rode in the back of Mr. Golf's sweet ride. It was a black Mercedes Benz with tinted windows. We were styling. It looked more and more like being a lawyer like Mr. Golf would be cool.

As we headed out of our neighborhood, Riana and I talked about what happened last night. We were both sad about the Thomas family.

"What happened?" Layah asked.

Though it was hard to keep talking about it, it actually made the time go by fast. The forty-five-minute drive from Chesterfield County to the north side of Richmond, Virginia, where Kings Dominion was located, flew by. Her dad was open and honest and told us that, sadly, adults don't always get along.

Mr. Golf said, "Sometimes folks need to be apart so that they can calmly think about their situation."

"Like you and Mom," Layah said in an irritated tone.

Her dad didn't reply. Riana and I looked at each other. She and I didn't want the tension to mount. But the car was as silent as if no one were there.

Layah looked out of the window with sad eyes. My heart felt bad for my friend. Not having your parents together had to be tough.

Riana whispered in my ear, "Carmen, we've just got to make this day really special since she misses her mom and stuff. We have to do whatever she wants to do all day, okay?"

I didn't make a comment. I wasn't sure if I wanted to do everything Layah wanted to do. Real friends make sure everyone is happy. But just to keep Riana off my back, I agreed.

The first few hours at the park, Riana's plan was working. Whatever Layah wanted to do, I was cool with. The three of us were having a ball. Mr. Golf was so funny on the rides, shouting like a big kid. Even though I was fine with riding what Layah wanted to ride, deep inside the Drop Ball was all I could think about.

The Drop Ball was a ride that went straight up and down. I had hoped that ride would be on her agenda so we wouldn't have any problems between us. Unfortunately, though, by the end of the day we had ridden everything except the Drop Ball.

It was almost ten o'clock and Mr. Golf told us this was going to be the last ride of the night, so we had to choose quickly. Layah wanted to ride on something that we had already ridden twice before. I had been hinting about getting on my ride every time we passed it. I was ignored.

I said with confidence, "Let's ride the Drop Ball now."

Layah insisted, "No, I don't want to ride that. We're not going to ride that. You guys are here with me. My dad paid for the tickets. We're not riding that."

She was so bossy. Not only did I scream out in frustration, but I pouted too.

When she and Riana lined up to ride the roller coaster for the third time, her dad sat with me. I couldn't hold back my tears.

Mr. Golf asked as he handed me one of the napkins from around his snow cone, "Carmen, you want to tell me what's wrong?"

"I only wanted to get on one ride in the whole place, just one," I confessed before blowing into the napkin. "Your daughter wouldn't let me. She is so mean sometimes, sir. And she takes over. I'm her friend and everything, but she makes me mad."

"I agree with you," he said between slurps. "You have every right to be angry with her. Layah invited you and Riana to come out here to this park to have a good time—not for you guys to just follow behind her and grant her every wish. I'm actually surprised you two let her lead all day long." `

I was glad Mr. Golf was with me on this. "Well, it was Riana's idea. She thought since Layah was sad about her mom and because this was a trip for her to help with her mom not being with her on Mother's Day and stuff, that we should be nice and do whatever she wants. I was fine with that, but I didn't think that Layah wouldn't let us choose one ride, you know?"

He nodded and said, "Well, that's very nice of you guys. You two are really good friends of hers to pick up on the fact that though she tries to be so tough, she is really sad that her mom is not constantly in her life. Carmen, I can't tell you not to be mad at Layah because she was wrong. She wasn't raised to be bossy."

I wanted Mr. Golf to give me some dap on that one. Layah had no reason to act pushy. Even her father thought I should stand my ground.

"But . . ." He switched tones, showing me that he was about to make an adult point. "I can tell you, if you can find it in that golden heart of yours to keep showing her grace, maybe you and Riana can help her really deal with her pain."

What was he saying to me? Did he want my help in getting Layah to admit that she still deeply missed her mom? I believed that until she said it bothered her, she could never ask for the help to move on.

He continued, "She cries herself to sleep some nights, Carmen. She picks up the phone to call her mom and almost every time she gets the answering machine. She goes into a store and wishes her mom were there to help pick out a nice dress. She comes away disappointed when she sees other girls her age shopping with their moms. I don't want to make excuses for Layah, but maybe we all need to help her see that she is hurting."

Wow, that was a lot. I never knew my tough friend was so wounded. As I listened to him, the anger I had for her was drifting away like a sailboat leaving the shore.

"Like me, I need to do better as a dad to tell her not to be so bossy. Particularly with two friends who really care about her, but understand, this time you are giving her will help her through Mother's Day. She'll be able to look back and remember the fun time she had with you guys here. Folks who are bossy usually aren't bossy by nature. They've got something else going on with them that they gotta work through. Good friends don't bail on them. They don't give up on them. Best pals try to help them get over the pain. Got me?" Mr. Golf asked as I nodded.

When my two friends came running talking about how much fun they'd had, I looked at Layah in silence and was actually excited to see a smile on her face. I couldn't imagine going through life without my mom. It hurt me that she was hurting like that. So what? I didn't get to ride the Drop Ball this time. I was able to help a friend, and that was more important.

As the three of us walked behind her dad toward the exit out of the park, we passed the Drop Ball one more time. Layah wrapped her arm around my shoulder and said, "Carmen, I didn't get on that ride because I was scared and I didn't want anybody to know that. I'm sorry I didn't let you get on your favorite ride. You're tougher than me."

Wow, I thought to myself as I smiled at my friend.

Layah was afraid to get on the Drop Ball and she called me tough. Now, I really couldn't be mad at her anymore.

This was a good night. I didn't come for me; I came to support Layah.

"Next time my family comes, I'll see if you can come with us, Layah. It's really no big deal."

Her dad looked back at us and said, "We've got time for one more ride. I know I told your parents I would have you home at eleven, but I'll call."

Layah hesitated. "Will you guys ride the Drop Ball with me?"

"I'm scared too," Riana said. "I'll watch you guys down here."

"No," I said, pulling both of them to the empty line. "We're buddies. We're going together hand in hand."

Minutes later, I held on tight to my girlfriends as we dropped down. At the same time we physically dropped, I also felt all the bossiness, meanness, and sadness drift away. We screamed screams of joy. How cool.

✪

When we got to school on Monday, there was a big assembly, and a bunch of important people were there from our county to talk about domestic violence. The incident in my neighborhood was something everybody wanted to talk about in class on Monday, so the principal called a

big assembly and brought professionals in to deal with
the difficult subject.

An important-looking man with a suit said, "Hello,
boys and girls. I'm Mr. Redmond and I'm here from the
Chesterfield County Hospital. I've been brought in today
to speak to you for a few minutes on the subject of domestic violence."

Though I knew I needed to learn more about the subject, I was squirming in my seat. *Why do I need to know
more about this tough issue?* I wanted the world to be perfect. However, I knew that wasn't realistic; and learning
as much as I could, even about the bad stuff, was a good
thing.

When Mr. Redmond introduced the short man
dressed in a karate suit to help him, the students looked
interested. The man started out with some karate moves.
His cool skills eased the whole atmosphere. He finished
by breaking a piece of wood with his hand. After that, we
were all ready to listen.

"Did you all like that demonstration?" Mr. Redmond
asked as he came back to the stage.

The cafeteria cheered collectively.

"Well, breaking that board in two is okay, but using
that same power to harm another person is not good.
First of all, I want you guys to know what domestic violence is. It occurs when there is a physical fight, or threatening argument, between family members. This might
take place between a husband and wife or any other

family members. In most cases the husband or male is the abuser. However, we have found incidents where the wife or female has been the abuser too.

"Anytime someone in the relationship uses verbal, mental, or physical abuse of any kind toward someone he or she is supposed to care for, that is also domestic violence."

As Mr. Redmond gave us the serious information, the students grew serious as well. I think a lot of kids were scared that maybe what happened to the Thomases could happen to them. We did need help, I guess. I mean, what is a kid to do if their parents fuss really, really bad? Maybe this lecture would show us the best way kids should respond.

"We want you to know that you don't have to be scared in your home. If you feel frightened about a situation in your home or someone's home that you're visiting, you should immediately call 9-1-1. If you or someone you know just needs to talk, call our hotline number, 1-800-NOABUSE, where counselors are waiting to speak confidentially with you. We want to get moms, dads, uncles, aunts, cousins, friends, neighbors, and anyone who needs it the help they need," Mr. Redmond said as he looked slowly around at all of us.

He gave us three important warning signs to look out for. One, if you are in your home and you hear adults arguing loud, someone threatening another, or stuff being thrown around the house, don't go in there and try to stop it; call the police. Two, when you hear one of the adults saying stop or begging the other one to leave them alone, call the police. Third, when you see one parent or person crying after an argument, saying they want to leave because they're scared, then you need to encourage that person to call the hotline themselves and get help.

In closing he said, "We can't help anyone who won't help themselves, but this is how we can help you help your family. We want your families to be happy and healthy. We want you to be aware, because domestic violence can start off small and end up big. It's nothing to laugh about. Know that it's okay to be aware of what it is. Seeking help for anyone who won't help themselves or encouraging your family member to seek help is a way to get through that dark hour."

2

Warm Moment

Beaches, sand, waves, cold lemonade, and bathing suits were all part of my exciting dream. I was laughing, imagining pouring sand all over my dad's head. Then in the dream, when he tried to catch me, he fell in the hole where Cassie had built a castle.

"Girl, what are you laughing at back there?" my dad asked, waking me up from my dream.

"Dad, I was dreaming about the family vacation, I guess. We were on the beach. It was so hot, so fun, and so cool. When are we going to Hilton Head?"

He laughed. "Carmen, you've only got two more weeks of school left. Just be patient. You'll be there in no time. We leave next month."

It was Mother's Day weekend and we were headed to North Carolina to see my grandparents. I didn't have anything against going, but I wanted to spend my weekend at home. Most of the weekend would be spent driving six hours there and then driving six hours back. However, I didn't complain.

The DVD we put in an hour ago was now watching us. I looked over to my left and Clay was snoring, and on my right, Cassie was fast asleep with her mouth wide open. They both looked funny.

At first, all the Browne kids had to keep my dad company on the ride because my mom had worked so hard on the paintings she was doing for the schools and the Pure Grace CD cover that she was asleep as soon as we hit the road. Pure Grace was my favorite gospel group. I even got a chance to sing on their CD. But not too long after we drove through Chick-fil-A, a fast-food restaurant, we all went to sleep as well.

"I knew y'all couldn't hang," my dad teased.

"Okay, I'm going to stay up. We'll have daddy-daughter time," I said, scooting up behind him. "So, how does the football team look this year?"

"I'm training you well," he said as we passed the car with a Florida license plate. "You've always loved football, Carmen, huh?"

"Yes, sir. So much that I wish I could play the game."

Chuckling lightly, he asked, "If you could play, what position would it be?"

"Guess, Dad," I said, playing with him.

He guessed every position but the one I'd strive to play. So I said, "None of those, Dad. I'd be the field kicker. They don't work as hard, but they have a big job."

"Do you think you'll try out for cheerleading in middle school?" he asked.

"Yeah, but I don't think I can try out until the end of sixth grade; so I still have a while before cheering, Dad. Guess I'll have to stick with cheering for VSU." He smiled at what I said.

At school there was a guy I sort of liked, but he had nothing on what I felt for my dad. I could never imagine loving a guy as much as I loved Charles Browne.

Finally, we arrived at his parents' house. As soon as we got there, Grandma Annabelle was there standing with open arms, hugging me tighter than I ever knew I could be hugged. Grandpa Harry asked for a peck on the cheek. It was good seeing both of them.

"Hey, Carmen, baby, now go on up there and get some sleep. Tomorrow we gonna head to the mall. I got so much stuff I want to buy for y'all," she said as I gave her a huge hug back.

She didn't have to tell me twice. Before I could say good night to anyone else, I hopped in the bed, ready for a big day at the mall. I guess shopping was my favorite thing to do.

✦

The next day ended up being so cool. My grandma Annabelle had such good taste, and she knew how to spoil all her grandchildren. She bought me some of the prettiest summer dresses and short sets I'd ever seen.

There was a phrase she always used to tell me. She'd say, "I'm not rich, but I worked hard enough back in the day so that in my old age I could have as much fun as I wanted, spending it on my grandkids."

Clay was so happy when he got some name-brand tennis shoes and clothes. I don't know what middle school had done to him, but he was into the "gear." Cassie got spoiled too. My parents kept telling my grandma she was doing too much for us. She didn't care though. It was Mother's Day weekend and she was giving us stuff. Finally, we took her to Red Lobster. It was her favorite restaurant in the entire world. She loved seafood and I did too. I remembered the first time she ever let me taste crab. *Ooh, it was so good.*

At dinner Grandma Annabelle said, "I hate that I won't be able to see you guys tomorrow. I know you've got to go to your other grandma's house. I just love showering my sweet babies with gifts. It fills me with joy."

Splitting our time between the two of them in Durham, North Carolina, was hard. Both grandmothers wanted all of our time. I had learned how to make the most of the time I spent with each one of them. Grandparents are dear people who had so much to teach me.

"Baby, I am so proud of you," she said as she looked over at my father. "You have a precious family, a lovely wife, adorable children, just . . . just . . . can't say enough. I'm just so proud of you, Mr. Head Coach."

My dad reached in his pocket and pulled out a beautiful shiny box. He told his mom that my mom had picked it out, and she smiled bashfully. I didn't know much about jewelry, but my grandma had introduced me to Tiffany & Company a few summers ago. She loved things from there. I recognized the pretty pale blue box with the white ribbon. I loved the way the three-diamond-stone necklace sparkled.

"Oh, a past, present, and future piece," Grandma said, taking the necklace from the box. "This is so sweet," she said as she looked at my parents.

"Well, I just thought of it this way," my mom said. "One stone represents all the things you do for us, Mama; another stands for the things you used to do, and the last stone is for all the things you're going to do. We love you so much. If it wasn't for you, Mama, I wouldn't have your son."

The next day at my mom's mother's house, things weren't so sweet. My mama and my grandma were fussing. My mom wanted to cook everything, but my grandma Lula liked things a certain way—old-fashioned southern cooking. I didn't care. I was just happy I didn't have to be in the kitchen. Then, when it was time to eat, we had to wait another hour for my auntie Chris and uncle Mark to arrive.

Boy, when they finally showed up, we all had mean looks on our faces. We were hungry! No one said hello.

My grandmother said something to them, though, and it wasn't pleasant. "I can't believe this Chris. You and your husband are so selfish. It's Mother's Day. Y'all were supposed to have been here. My food's getting cold. Getting here this late, you could have stayed away."

My aunt gave her husband a very mean stare. If looks could hurt, then somebody would be in the hospital. Unfortunately, the way Auntie Chris stared him down made Uncle Mark really upset.

My uncle said harshly, "Chris, don't be looking at me that way. I told you to go on. You decided to wait. I didn't ask you or tell you to, and if you give me any more drama, you gon' be here with your family by yourself."

Uncle Mark went storming off to the bathroom. My aunt's eyes were watering. I felt really bad for her. She couldn't look at us. Her husband had embarrassed her in front of all her family. I hated to see what would happen if he really got angry.

My grandma put her arm around her daughter. We prayed and started eating without Uncle Mark. When he finally came to the table about fifteen minutes later, the tension was thick, so thick that a knife couldn't even cut it. This Mother's Day was not going well.

I tried to break all the silence and said, "Auntie, Grandma, Mommy, happy Mother's Day. I love you all."

They all smiled at me and I knew, though we weren't the perfect family, I wouldn't trade them in for anything. Seeing them smile made my heart feel good.

✪

"Layah," I said to my friend the next week as she looked so pitiful, "what's wrong?"

"We have two more weeks of school, and I'm sad," my usually tough friend replied.

"School will be out soon. Next year we'll be going to middle school. Come on, girl, this is a good thing. No sad faces, okay?" I said to both Layah and Riana.

"I'm going to miss you guys," Layah said as she put her arms around our necks. "I know I'm supposed to be the tough one, but this year I really changed. I'm really into girl friendships. But I won't see my two buddies much anymore. You guys live right down the street from each other, so you'll see a lot of each other. It's just me and my dad. Besides you two, I don't hang with anyone. I don't want fifth grade to be over."

My friend was serious. I handed her a tissue to catch the tears streaming down her face. I let her know that the three of us had a bond that wouldn't be broken.

"Girl, don't sweat it. Whenever you wanna see us,

we'll be around. Plus, I know you're tired of me and Riana anyway," I said as the three of us laughed.

Having these friends was a blessing. I hadn't even thought about missing them over the summer because I was so tired of school. I'd be thrilled to have a break for a while. Now that Layah had brought it to my attention, I was truly going to miss my friends. Even though I had two siblings at home, having friends was different.

After school that day I was minding my own business, sitting downstairs in the family room in the recliner chair. As I channel surfed, I was enjoying watching a little bit of everything that my parents would approve of—going back and forth from Nickelodeon to Disney to the Family Channel to PBS. With school ending soon, we were just reviewing for exams, and I wasn't a whiz or anything, but after I studied a bit Mom said I could watch some TV.

All of a sudden, Clay walked in and snatched the remote out of my hand! He jumped on the couch, crossed his legs, and turned repeatedly to channels I didn't want to see. He kept going to ESPN and to some car mechanic show. *Ooooh, my brother is driving me crazy.* He never once looked over to see how much steam was coming out of my ears. Then he turned to some reruns of an old show called *Good Times.* He laughed wildly at this painter dude named JJ.

Am I going to let him boss me around and take the remote and have his way? I asked myself.

No way! I quickly stood to my feet, put my hands on

my hips, and stomped over to my brother. I leaned over him to grab the remote, but he yanked his hand back, waving it far out of my reach.

"Clay," I whined, "this is my time. I was sitting here watching TV. That's not fair. You can't take the remote."

"Blah, blah, blah, my sister is saying something, but I can't hear her. Blah, blah, blah," he teased. "Tell ya what, if you can get the remote, you can change the channel."

He ran around to the other side of the couch. I tried to catch him and take the remote, but I was too slow. When I saw I couldn't outrun my brother, I took a coaster from the table and swung it at him. It hit him right above the eye.

"Ouch, girl! See, I was gon' give it back to you. Now I'm going to watch TV," Clay said in a defiant way.

He held his forehead with one hand and gripped the remote to his chest with the other. Then he said in pain, "You were down here watching TV; now I want to watch TV before Cassie comes down here and starts bothering me. Carmen, you gotta share, girl."

He had a point, but I had only been watching for a few minutes. The way we handled TV watching was, whoever was in the family room first decided what we would watch all the way up until dinnertime.

How did Clay get to decide he was going to change the rules? How could Clay be so mean to me? I'd gone out on a limb for him recently. A month ago I helped him find information about his birth parents. When nobody else would help him, I was there. I was his sister, his little sister, for crying out loud, his sister that he owed something to, his sister that he didn't have any right to boss around. The more I thought about it, the madder I got.

When a tear dropped down my face, he looked over at me and said, "That's not going to make me give you the remote. Toughen up, girl. Go bother one of your friends on the phone or go play with a doll or something. I was just playing with you at first and then you gonna throw something at me. You're not gettin' no remote back now Sis, sorry."

"I'ma tell Mama," I said to him.

"And what you gon' tell her? You'll be the one in trouble when I tell her that you threw something at me. Plus, my head hurts," he said, acting like I'd really gotten him good.

He had another point there. But no way could I let him boss me around and get away with it. I headed upstairs to sulk.

As I got halfway up my brother taunted, "Hey, Carmen, I'll call you when and if I'm done, *maybe*."

I had to pass by the kitchen to get to my room at the end of the hall. My mom was in there stirring up the best Italian sauce I'd smelled in ages. With a long, gloomy look on my face, I pitifully walked into the kitchen and grabbed a few cookies and some milk.

"Is this snack okay, Mom?" I asked slowly.

"That's fine, honey. What's the matter with you? I thought you were watching TV."

"My brother gets on my nerves. I wish he'd go back to wherever he came from."

Harshly she scolded, "Carmen Browne, we don't joke like that—understand?"

"I'm sorry, Mom, but Clay does get on my nerves. He was down there telling me what to do. He won't even let me watch TV and I was there first."

"That boy," my mom said as she placed the spoon on the stove.

My mom started to leave the kitchen, and I knew she was going downstairs to set Clay straight.

"No, no, no," I said, stopping her on her way.

With her hand on her hip, she asked, "Why don't you want me to go downstairs to talk to Clay? What is he going to tell me? Did you do something, Carmen?"

Nodding, I said, "I threw a coaster at him, but I wasn't trying to fight him or anything like that."

My mom told me that I'd better not throw anything at anyone anymore. I told her I understood and then she asked me to have a seat at the kitchen table. Knowing there was something deeper going on with me, she questioned me until I told her why I was so frustrated.

"Why do some people have to have their way all the time? Clay just bossed me around, and it even happened at Kings Dominion a couple weeks back. Layah was bossy too."

My mom cut me off and said, "Young lady, you are bossy sometimes as well." I looked at her as if she'd misspoken. "Come on, admit it, dear."

"Okay, maybe sometimes I want to have things my way," I blurted out.

"Well, then I'm glad you've experienced how it feels when someone is too pushy. Because of how Clay and Layah treated you recently, you have a better sense of how to treat others. And I'll speak to your brother about his behavior as well, though. Carmen, again, I can't stress it enough. You've got to treat people the way you want to be treated," my mom said, kissing me as I headed out of the kitchen.

✪

"Go, Carmen, go! We can beat the boys!" I heard Layah yell as I hopped in the potato sack and tried to win the race on field day a week later.

I hopped and hopped and crossed the finish line before the boys in my class. Excitement made my knees start shaking, and my two friends came up and hugged me tight. We jumped up and down for joy. At the three-legged race it was my turn to sit on the sidelines. Layah and Riana were tied together, and I had to cheer them on as hard as they cheered for me.

I was interrupted from watching when Spencer Webb or "Spence," as we called him, startled me and said,

"Tomorrow is the last day of school. My granddad told me that he was going to have your family over for dinner soon. I hope you come; that way I'll see you."

My dad hadn't said anything about going to eat at his boss's house. But I hoped that we were going because Spence was a guy I was fond of, and getting to see him over the summer would be cool.

"That's cool," I said before moving my head so I could finish watching the race. "Can't talk right now, though, Spence; the girls are killing the boys. We just won another race. Yeah!"

At the end of the day the girls had won more races than the boys had. We took first place. Tomorrow there would be a pizza party to celebrate. Layah, Riana, and I couldn't stop shouting. But to top off that excitement, we had a water balloon fight with no winners or losers. It was just pure fun. Ten minutes later, we were all soaked.

I saw Layah and Riana drenched and I realized we were only going to have one more day of this. I got a little down. Last week Layah felt like this and I acted like it wasn't a big deal. Well, it was. I was going to miss our time together.

"Why are you looking so sad?" my mom asked me later that evening when we went shopping for Miss Pryor's gift. "Tomorrow is the last day of school. You're supposed to be excited about that."

"I'm just going to miss my friends, that's all," I said as we headed to the cash register to buy a nice lotion set.

"Well, that's understandable. I'm glad God sent you good friends. We'll think of some creative things to do with them this summer, and Riana's just down the street. You're going to be fine."

On the way home my mom told me I needed to treasure all the memories of being in elementary school, from where we used to live in Charlesville to our home in Ettrick now. Take all the lessons that I learned, particularly in the fifth grade, and be smarter in middle school. I heard everything she said, but I still wasn't happy.

At the next red light I said, "I enjoyed my class this year, and next year I'll have so many classes; who knows if I'll have any classes with Layah or Riana again. I hate change, Mom."

"Oh, come on, Carmen. Change isn't bad. It's sort of how you look at things. You know what I always say: The glass is half full. You have to look at it from a positive angle. Next year you will be going on to bigger and better things. I know it might seem a little scary, but don't worry about that, sweetie; you're going to do great. You're going to be fine. You're going to be dynamite. Yes, there will be some changes, but change is a good thing. You will always have the past to treasure and build on."

Still needing more advice, I asked, "But what if we're not in class together next year, Mom?"

"You're not in class with your old buddy Jillian anymore, and you guys are still friends," she reminded me.

I giggled slightly. "That's true. I should call her."

I loved that my mom was always there. Since I was going to middle school, I knew I was going to have to lean on her for so much. This pre–middle school talk let me know that I was going to be able to tell her anything. It was a good conversation.

The next day at school, I tried as hard as I could not to be upset, but I was. And I wasn't the only one; we were all excited to get our yearbooks signed and enjoy a pizza party. As the day drew to a close, the reality of change hit me. Miss Pryor gave us time to talk as long as we agreed not to be rambunctious. She loved the album I gave her as a thank-you gift. It was engraved on the front.

"Layah, I owe you an apology," I said to my girlfriend.

"For what? You didn't do anything to me."

"Yeah, I did. Last week I told you it wasn't a big deal that we wouldn't be in school together anymore. I wasn't sensitive to your feelings, 'cause now I'm really sad. I'm going to miss both of you guys. Yeah, Riana is just down the street, but she has a lot of activities like I do, and who knows when we're going to see each other," I said to my two friends.

The three of us held hands. We got teary eyes. I had to be real and tell them what they meant to me.

"I love you guys. I didn't want to move here at all, but because I met you two, I love it here now."

Layah chimed in. "I never really liked girls. Hanging around them and playing with them wasn't my thing until you guys came along. I talked to my dad and he said that maybe we could do more things together this summer."

"Now what if we go to middle school next year and we never even talk to each other?" Riana said, putting a damper on the whole situation. "Carmen, I really didn't have any friends until you came. What if it's that way next year and the two of you guys find new friends?"

"It's not going to be that way. We have our own special sisterhood now. Nobody or nothing is going to break it," I said as we hugged.

Later that day, the three of us ate our pizza over in the corner. Miss Pryor was making her way over to sign everybody's yearbook. When she came over to us, we had long faces. I didn't know why we were so sad. We had talked about how we weren't going to be together in sixth grade but that we would still be friends. For some reason our hearts were still hurting.

"Well, if it isn't my three little musketeers over here in this corner. What in the world is going on?" Miss Pryor asked as she took her hand and lifted up my chin.

I couldn't answer her. She just had to figure it out. There was just no way to make us happy. We didn't want things to change, bottom line.

Miss Pryor was happy because she was engaged and getting married soon. Her change was a good change. But when she said she was proud of all three of us, we perked up a little.

"At the beginning of the school year, Carmen, you

were new and hoping to find your way. Riana, you were so shy you never answered any questions in class. And, Miss Layah, well, girl, you were such a bully. But the three of you all are good together, a great balance. You did something special in your friendship. Friendships are very important. You guys have learned how to share, you've taught each other things, and you've made a difference in each other's lives."

Hearing her say that was encouraging. Miss Pryor was the best teacher I'd ever had. She knew how to relate to her students.

"You may think you're too grown sometimes. Your parents told me about your disobedience in the mall incident, but you learned so much this year. Look at me, ladies," she said as she noticed our heads down. "Don't think about what you might not have anymore; think about how strong you are academically, how happy you are for each other as friends, and how proud your parents are of you guys. I'll tell you a little secret. You guys are my favorite students. I enjoyed watching your friendship mature into something special. I still have some of my same friends from elementary school. A few of them will be my bridesmaids. And you all can be the same way too. You have that special ingredient of caring that's going to make your friendship last and last. So put some smiles on your faces."

We all hugged her. We didn't want to leave her either. She was the bomb.

"Don't worry, I'll be checking up on you. My fiancé just got a job at your school. He'll be the new gym teacher, so I'll see you ladies every now and then, and when I do, I know you're going to make me proud."

She was right; we did have a lot to be happy about. We said it to each other; my mom had said it—now we just had to believe it. I looked at the two of them and they responded with big smiles. I just knew our friendship would stay intact.

We had a group hug and Miss Pryor said, "Wait, let me go get my camera. I have to take this picture to put in my new album. It's a true picture of friendship. This is a warm moment."

3

Pushy Ways

Layah, I can't believe you're going to your grandmother's for the whole summer. I mean, you were the one who talked about spending time with Riana and me, and now you're going to be gone for the whole summer. That's not cool," I said into the receiver as the three of us talked on three-way.

"I'm just sad," Riana chimed in, "our little group is breaking up. Maybe I can ask my mom if I can have a slumber party before you jet out of here, Layah. Do you think you guys can come?"

"Well, my family doesn't have anything planned," I cut in and said. "But I certainly can't speak for my mom. I have to ask. I'm sure it won't be a problem. I'm right down the street."

"I don't know if I can come," Layah said. "I'm going to be down there for a while, so I really just want to spend time with my dad before I go."

"So you're saying no," I said to her in an abrupt way.

I didn't know what was happening to me. Lately, I was getting really short with my friends. I didn't mean to be so bossy, but whatever I was feeling on the inside was just kinda coming out on the outside. I didn't do a good job of controlling how it was coming out, and it sounded kinda bad.

"All right, all right, all right," Layah said. "I'll see what I can do. I wanna hang out with you guys too, and I'm sort of sad that I'm leaving. But I don't have a mom like you guys and my grandma wants to spend time with me. I want to be with her too."

"Why now?" Riana asked.

"I sort of feel my body changing and I want to be around my granny, that's all. It's not that I don't wanna be around you guys. I love you two. I'm sure my dad will let me come," Layah said.

After I got off the phone with them, I thought about the fact that I had no plans for the summer. Boy, did I hate that I had boxed my teddy bear up. He and I could have a really good conversation right about now. He could help me figure out why my life was so dull and boring.

My dad would be busy with football camp and my

mom would be working on her mural projects. Since Clay would be playing football for our eighth-grade team next year, he, too, was going to be busy with summer work-outs. Cassie would have gymnastics camp every day. I was bummed out that everyone had something to do but me. *Why didn't I have plans?*

I went downstairs and saw my mom's pretty picture of the coolest cougar I had ever seen. It was a middle school mascot. I gave her a thumbs-up, making sure I didn't say a word when I noticed her on the phone. She motioned for me to come to her.

"Sweetie, it's your auntie; she wants to speak to you."

Wow, I thought before taking the phone. I missed my aunt and certainly hoped she was okay. The last time I saw her, she and my uncle were disagreeing pretty heavily.

"Hey, lady," she said excitedly.

"Hey, Auntie," I said happy, to hear her sound so good.

"Since I'm a teacher, you know I have the summer off. I couldn't get you guys down here last year because y'all were moving, packing boxes, and getting settled in your new home. But I was just talking to your mom and I'd really like it if you and Cassie could come down here and stay with me for a week this summer. That sound okay?"

"Oh, my gosh!" I said with my eyes getting all big, forgetting any problem she may or may not have. "Yeah, I would love to stay with you!"

My aunt was the coolest. The thought of spending

time with her gave me something to look forward to. Although I wanted to stay longer than a week, seven days away from here was sounding really good. *North Carolina, here I come.*

"Well, don't get excited too fast," my mom said to me. "I gotta run it by your dad. I know he has something planned for us. After everything we went through with Clay and the adoption stuff, we just need to take a couple of family vacations."

"Vacations—we're going somewhere other than Hilton Head?"

"Maybe, we are," she said.

My summer was looking up more and more. "When are we going? How long are we staying? What places are we going to?" I asked, out of breath.

"Carmen, calm down," my auntie Chris said. "I know you're excited about the summer. Maybe your parents can work it out for you and Cassie to come visit."

"I thought Cassie was in that tumbling camp?"

"Yeah, but your mom said she could miss if your dad said it was okay."

Quickly I thought hanging with Cassie in Durham would probably give us a chance to grow closer. I wouldn't be able to look out for her anymore in elementary school. Now Clay would sort of be looking out for me, though I didn't need him to.

I'd be the little person at middle school. I needed to make sure my sister was prepared for the fourth grade. So the plan to see my aunt and my grandparents at the same time was a delight.

"I'm in," I said to her.

"Great, baby, we'll have a ball. Give your mom the phone," she voiced.

❂

My parents' bedroom was beside mine, and later that evening I was so bummed out when I heard my dad say, "No way they're going down there without us. They can visit your sister when we're all down there. A week, no, that's too long."

"Charles, the girls really want to go."

"Honey, I said no and that's final," my dad said harshly.

Sitting on my bed, upset about what I'd overheard I thought, *Why do my plans always have to get messed up? Why can't stuff go right for me? Why did my dad have to be set on ruining everything? I don't want to be around here all summer long. I should have known not to get too excited.*

Things weren't all bad. Two days later, Layah and I were at Riana's house for the big sleepover. This was the first all-nighter we'd been allowed to have since our little excursion to the mall that didn't go too well. Boy, did we learn not to disobey our parents. We learned that we needed to be open and honest about everything.

"So do you guys wanna watch a movie? You wanna

play Xbox? Or do my favorite thing and play Barbie dolls?" Riana asked.

"Barbie dolls?" Layah said. "Please, that's for kids. We're going to middle school."

Though I didn't play Barbies with Cassie anymore, I wouldn't mind pretending I was younger. Playing with Barbies allowed me to do that. But I hadn't touched them in a couple of years. I didn't want to make Riana feel like her idea was stupid, so I sort of stayed neutral and didn't say anything either way.

Layah stood on Riana's bed and said, "I wanna play *Need 4 Speed* car racing game. I wanna beat you guys at something. I came to have fun, not watch TV. I could have done that at home and I certainly don't wanna play with a Barbie doll."

When I thought about it, I didn't wanna play Xbox. Though the Barbie idea was something I wasn't opposed to, I wasn't really feeling it either. A movie—a cool Disney movie with high school girls in it—that would be relaxing and fun. And being able to watch something with my friends would be "tight."

So I tried convincing my friends by saying, "I'm for TV. We can pop some popcorn, watch a movie . . . yeah, let's do that."

I hoped I would get them excited about what I wanted to do. No one was budging. They didn't like my suggestion and I didn't like theirs. They didn't want each other's suggestions either. We were in three different corners of

Riana's room, with three different viewpoints on how we wanted to spend the evening. This was going to be a long night. The thrill was gone early on.

"Okay, guys," I finally broke down and said. "We're being selfish here; everybody wants to do their own thing. How about we do all of them?"

"Okay, okay," Riana said. "I would be willing to do that."

"Play dolls and watch a girly movie? I don't know." Layah hesitated.

"Come on, Layah, it's only fair," Riana told her.

"All right, cool," Layah said, giving in.

The next big issue was which activity we would do first.

"Well, it's my house, so I think we should play dolls first," Riana popped up and said firmly.

I actually couldn't believe my timid friend had a little backbone. When I first met her last year, she was so shy and soft-spoken that whatever I wanted to do, she was all for it.

But I had to show her manners. So I said, "No, we're the guests, so you should be hospitable and let us go first with the things we want to do, then if there's time . . ."

"If there's time?" Layah said, stepping beside Riana. "That's not right, Carmen; we just all agreed that we were going to do everybody's equally."

"Well, the movie might run long; I mean, it's two hours," I told them, hoping they'd understand.

"No, no, no," Layah said, placing her hand in my face. "I hope you don't think we're going to play Xbox for thirty minutes, play dolls for an hour and watch your movie for two hours. Riana's mom ain't gonna let us stay up all night long," she said, moving her neck from side to side.

"Yeah, Carmen," Riana chimed in. "We've only got three hours before my mom is going to make us go to bed, so that means an hour for each of the three things. So maybe you can go downstairs, surf through the channels, and find something good that we might want to see that's only one hour long. I'll set up the dollhouse and pull out all my Barbie dolls. Layah, you can go ask my brother if he'll let us borrow his Xbox. You guys come back to my room in five minutes, and then we'll figure out which is first, second, and third. Cool?"

"Sounds good to me," Layah said when I didn't respond. "Oh, you'll get over it, Carmen. This is the way we're doing it."

Layah spoke to me in a very mean way, not caring that her tone was truly hurting my feelings. But I didn't cry. I accepted that I wasn't going to have my way.

When I walked downstairs, I was surprised to see Riana's little sister, Rolanda, watching the cartoon channel. *This isn't good.* I had to get her away from the TV so I could find a show.

"Hey," I said, being really nice so she would let me turn to the TV-guide channel.

"Oh, hey, Carmen."

"Whatcha doin'?" I asked in a really jovial voice.

"Can't you see, I'm watching TV," she shot back as annoyingly as my own little sister can be sometimes.

This was going to be harder than I thought. All little sisters seemed like they were just alike, little pests. *How am I going to get the remote?*

"What do you want? I'm trying to watch TV and you're buggin' me," Rolanda said.

"Umm, I was just sorta hoping I could borrow the remote for a second. We're gonna watch TV later, and I want to see what's coming on," I said, smiling.

"You wanna watch TV. *Please.* I don't have any friends over. Riana has you and that other girl."

"Her name is Layah."

"Whatever."

Rolanda kept shaking her head from side to side and the beads were quite annoying, but I guess she wanted me to comment on her new do. "Your hair is really pretty."

"Don't try to butter me up. I'm not going to leave the TV. My mom said I could watch it 'til it was time to go to bed."

"What time do you have to go to bed?" I asked, hoping we could watch the movie once she was done.

Rolanda replied, tightly holding the control, "Same time you guys do; that's a dumb question."

Cassie wanted to come over here with me to spend the night with Rolanda, but I told my mom I needed my own time with my friends without Cassie running in and out of the room all night. Now I was seriously regretting that decision. If Cassie were here, the two of them would probably be playing in Rolanda's room, and I would be able to at least flip through the channels to see if there was something on I would wanna see. This was a nightmare.

When I hurried back upstairs, the two of them were playing dolls. They didn't seem to miss me at all. The fact that they started without me was tough to take.

"What took you so long?" Riana asked me.

"It's your sister; she won't even let me look at the TV guide to see any other channels."

Layah started laughing. "Oh, so you can't even check. Well, come and play dolls with us. We get to play Xbox in an hour."

"So it doesn't even matter if I would have found a movie," I whined. "You guys already started playing dolls and you're saying Xbox is next. I thought we were going to decide which order we were going to go in when all of us got back in this room. You all decided without me. What's up with that?"

"It took you too long to come back in here, and it doesn't matter anyway," Layah said to me. "Her sister is watching TV."

"You know what, I don't want to play either one. Keep playing without me," I said in a whining tone.

"We will," Layah said sternly.

"Fine with us," Riana agreed.

I ran downstairs to their living room and just cried. I couldn't believe my two friends were so mean to me. Mrs. Anderson overheard me from the kitchen and sat down beside me. I turned away. She didn't give up, though.

"You gotta tell me what's wrong, sweetheart. Do you wanna go home?" Mrs. Anderson asked.

"No, ma'am, it's just my friends. We had decided what we were going to do and they started without me. I'm just sad because they don't even care that I don't wanna do what they wanna do. I can't believe they don't understand."

"Well, Carmen, let me just tell you," she said as she placed her arm around my shoulder, trying to cheer me up. "I've listened to you all off and on all night. I didn't interfere, but you guys have been using pretty harsh tones with each other. Friends shouldn't talk to each other in such mean ways like you girls sometimes do. You girls have been pretty bossy. Everybody wanting to have their own way. Real friendship is give-and-take. It's okay to be strong-willed sometimes, though."

Not quite understanding what she meant, she explained that strong-willed meant being determined and having leadership qualities.

Riana's mom said, "Sometimes in a friendship everybody is strong, and in order for them to get along someone has to give in. Everybody can't be pushy. Everybody can't be the boss. Somebody's got to follow. Someone's got to make the harmony happen."

I held my head down and thought about all she'd said. I was strong, but was I using my strength the right way by pouting? I knew the answer to that question was no.

She looked at me and said, "Maybe tonight your job is to be the bigger friend and give in to what the others want to do. Let me tell you, Carmen, Riana didn't have any real friends until you came along. And I've been see-ing Layah Golf for a couple of years, and she didn't like hanging out with girls at all until you showed up. So you've been a leader, Carmen Browne. In just the few months you've been here, you've made a difference."

My eyes were sparkling with pride. I had helped two girls become better people. Now that they weren't follow-ing me, I was hurt, when all along I'd helped them to grow.

Mrs. Anderson was right on when she continued, "You wanted them to shine. You've made them feel like they could show another side of themselves. Let them do that. You can still lead by showing them how one is sup-posed to act when one doesn't get his or her way."

I nodded, completely understanding what she was saying. Not only did I understand; I agreed. Walking back to Riana's room, I had learned a really good lesson. Enjoy-ing them wasn't about being right or being the boss; it was about being a real friend to make sure we all were happy. I was glad to go back to Riana and Layah. I went into the room with a big smile on my face and a new atti-tude. I knew tonight was going to be da bomb.

We played dolls, then Xbox, and when Rolanda went to sleep, Mrs. Anderson let us stay up a little bit longer and watch a movie after all. I wasn't expecting that, but it happened. Compromising was a cool thing. Before we went to bed, we said our prayers silently. I thanked God for helping me through my disappointment. It was cool that He was watching out for me.

✪

Two weeks had gone by since I had hung out with my friends and I missed them. Both were safely on their summer vacations. I had gotten a letter from Riana and a message on the answering machine from Layah. They both said that they were doing really good and missed me. My friends were missed in return.

My summer was not as boring as I thought it would be. I was helping my mother. I was sort of her assistant three days a week. The other two days a week were spent in NYSP, a National Youth Sports Program, at Virginia State. It was so fun because I worked with college cheerleaders.

Half of the morning we would work on educational stuff, preparing us for the upcoming school year, and the other half was recreation. I learned some of the coolest moves. Hanging out with the big girls was fun.

✪

Butterflies were flying around in my stomach as we headed to President Webb's home for a big dinner. I hadn't seen Spence since school was out. Since I couldn't talk to boys on the phone, I didn't know if he was going to be there or not. I remembered the last few days of school; he had mentioned something about seeing me again.

I put on my dress, a cute one that was black at the top and had a polka-dotted pink skirt attached at the bottom. I had cute black sandals to match.

Riding in the car, my dad gave us the family "Please don't embarrass me speech." "Now, I want you guys to be on your best behavior," he said, looking back at Clay, Cassie and me. "If you don't know which fork or spoon or whatever to use, look at your mom; she'll give you a heads-up. Remember to put the napkin in your lap, no elbows on the table, and it shouldn't be long, because President Webb is quick about business. So we should eat and be out of there in an hour; then I'll take you all for some ice cream. He's my boss, guys. . . ."

"All right, all right, Daddy, we got ya," Cassie said from the seat directly behind him. "We won't let you down."

"All right then," my dad said. We knew he wanted to make a good impression on his boss.

My mom chimed in next. "Everything will be fine."

I was all set to make my dad proud, ready to be on my best behavior, and to think about every move before I actually made it, but when we hit the beautiful mansion door and Spence opened it, I clammed up.

"Coach Browne, come on in, my good man," I heard President Webb say in a distinguished voice, as my dad had to coax me through the door.

"Carmen, come on, honey," my father said, gently pushing me, not realizing my feet were frozen.

Spence stared at me, smiling really wide, and I didn't know how to take that. I liked it but it felt weird. And of course I was real embarrassed when I tripped over my feet from my father nudging me through the door.

My father introduced us. "Sir, you remember my kids, Clay, my oldest, and my daughters, Carmen and then Cassie."

"Yes, what lovely kids you have, and, Carmen, I hear a lot of things about you from my grandson," President Webb said as I blushed again.

"Thanks for telling me, Dr. Webb; I'm going to look out for this guy," my father said as he punched Spence lightly in the arm.

Everyone laughed. Spence's grandmother was so beautiful. She had the prettiest gray hair I had ever seen. She welcomed us all into her home, and we immediately sat down at the long dining room table and began a scrumptious meal. Spence sat beside me. Neither of us said a word. We just listened to the adults talk.

When dinner was over, Spence took us to a playroom.
It was then that I realized that he lived with his grandparents. Spence turned on the Xbox and tried to teach me
how to play. There were two other joysticks that my
brother and sister were using. I didn't know if he knew
that we had Xbox too or what, but I grabbed the game
piece from him and said, "I don't know who you think
you're dealing with, but we have some of this stuff at
home. Yeah, we don't live in a mansion or whatever, but
we're not poor. We know how to play Xbox." So I went on
and on for a few more minutes, not realizing that I was
going overboard and being very harsh to Spence. My
brother and sister both looked at me as if to say "stop it."

In the middle Spence said, "Hey, I'm sorry, Carmen. I
wasn't trying to make you feel like I'm better than you or
anything. I think you're really cool. Well, I used to. I just
wanted to make sure you knew how to play the game. I
didn't want to be unfair. You don't have to worry about
me trying to help you anymore. Girl, you're got too many
pushy ways."

4

Nice Time

June was such a great month, for so many reasons. My birthday was just a month away, school was out, my family vacation was coming up, and I was getting personal time with my dad. Yep, I liked June.

My dad had made plans to take each of his three children out, to spend some quality time with them. He took Clay to Hampton, Virginia, to see the Harlem Globetrotters, a cool basketball team that did amazing tricks on the court. Cassie's outing with him was to Richmond, Virginia. They went to the civic center to see a play called *The Wiz*. My dad had taken her to see a real Broadway rendition of the play she was in on VSU's campus. Both my siblings came back saying how much fun they had with Dad.

Now it was my turn! And I didn't know where he was taking me. All I knew was that I had to be ready at six o'clock, and look my Sunday best. At five-fifty I was standing at the front door, ready to go.

"Mom, do you know where he's taking me?" I asked her as she stood with me, fixing my dress and ponytail.

"I'm sworn to secrecy. I can only tell you that you'll have a great time," she said. Though I wanted to know really badly, it didn't matter. My dad was taking me out on a date. Before I could explode from excitement, he came to the door, looking so sharp. My father was sporting a new suit and tie.

"We must be going somewhere fancy, huh?" I asked, nodding approval at his black suit, peach shirt, and tie that coordinated.

"Your old man look good?" my dad questioned as he twirled around.

"Real good," I said to him while giving him a hug around his waist.

He kissed my mom and we were headed out the door. Having my dad take me on this special date was cool enough. He always told me he loved me, but this date thing said those words in a whole new way.

"Hmm, I wonder what I have planned for my little lady?" he teased in between his whistling while we drove toward the next town over.

"Daddy . . . tell me," I said in a fun, whining way. "I've been wanting to know all day what we're gonna do."

"Okay, okay, I guess I won't keep you in suspense any longer," he said as he patted me on the head. "You're such a wonderful daughter, Carmen. Your mom and I are so blessed to have such beautiful kids. I am excited to show you off tonight. First we're going to dine at the Cordon Bleu."

"That really fancy restaurant that you and mom go to over in Petersburg?" I asked as he nodded. "Wow, I get to use my table etiquette. I've got to remember to use the silverware from the outside in."

"Sounds right to me. I need the practice as well. As head coach, the president has me attending a lot of fancy dinners. But that's not all, sweetie. That's just the start of our night on the town."

"Really, where else are we going?" I asked in anticipation.

"Your favorite group is in town ministering at Petersburg High School this evening. My buddy made sure we had front-row seats."

"Dad, are you serious? Pure Grace is here? They have been blowing up the gospel charts. I thought they completely forgot about me," I stated, knowing the group was so busy.

"Nope, they haven't forgotten about their special songbird. We're going to have dessert with them backstage after the concert. You ready to have some fun with your pops?" he asked.

"Very ready, Dad," I said, so overjoyed.

Looking up at the sky that was growing darker by the minute, I just thanked God for the time with my father. He was so busy, yet he looked forward to his time off from coaching to spend time with his family.

I missed our talks. I'd been talking to my mom so much lately that she knew all about me. My thoughts, the things that scared me, the things that made me smile. In a way, my dad didn't know much about me at all anymore. I didn't even know if he really knew my girlfriends' names. But now we'd get a chance to catch up. As he played Pure Grace's CD, we rode in sweet silence.

Though I wanted to talk to him, I really didn't know what I wanted to talk about. So maybe music was a good distraction to make up for the silence.

"You're awfully quiet," my father said to me at dinner as I cut into my medium-well steak.

I just looked at him. My dad was perfect to me. I was happy that he got his dream job. I hoped he'd have a winning team this season. I knew that if he didn't, he'd probably lose his job.

"I'm okay, Dad. Just happy to be out with you. You're quiet too," I said, springing it all back on him.

"Yeah, you're right. There's something that I've been meaning to ask you, but your dad's a little nervous about it," he said, playing with his collar as if it were too tight.

What has him all nervous? My dad had never been that way when it came to conversations with me. *Why is he acting weird?*

Intrigued I asked, "Yes, Daddy? What do you want to know?"

I put down my utensils and gave him my undivided attention. "I want to talk about boys. One in particular. Tell me about this Spence guy. What's going on there? Do you think guys are cool now? Understand I'm not mad or anything. I just want you to talk to me. What's going on with you, Carmen?"

Okay, quickly I felt weird. I had to drink some water and look away. My dad brought up a subject I wasn't expecting at all. I admitted that I did think Spence was extra cool. I also mentioned that I thought Spence was mad at me because I was rather pushy when we went to his house for dinner.

My dad chuckled and said, "You're a bossy little lady, huh? Well, Carmen, if you ever want to talk about your feelings, you can do that with me. I love you and you're special. Everything about you is precious, and I don't want you to ever rush your youth. It's okay to think that boys are cool, but right now concentrate on school and hanging out with your girlfriends, Layah and Riana," he said, surprising me that he knew their names.

He went on to tell me that he's always there for me to talk to. He said that later in high school he and Mom would explain more about what dating God's way means. He also said he wasn't going to allow me to date for a long time, years, but that if I ever had questions, he and my mom were there.

"Carmen, here's my first lesson on that subject. Most guys like to pursue a young lady. They don't want the girl following them, calling them all the time, or so into them that it makes them feel smothered. So keep your feelings in check, whatever they may be."

"Dad, I really don't like him like that, nothing big or anything. I don't kiss him or nothing." I couldn't believe I said that, but I was being honest, even though it made my dad almost choke.

"I'm okay," he replied, noticing my eyes were wide. "I'm glad you don't want to kiss him or anything. Just remember this talk we're having. After God, I'm your number one man. All the other jokers, and I know there will be many because you're a great girl . . ."

"All the other guys, Dad, could never compare to you and God," I said, touching his hand that was on top of the table. "No guy will ever take your place, Dad."

"Maybe one day about ten or fifteen years from now, you'll change your mind on that," he said, sort of laughing. "But until that time, keep talking to your mom. Keep talking to me. Especially keep talking to God. The three of us have your back."

I understood and we hugged. We finished our delicious dinner and went to see Pure Grace. They even let me sing a little harmony backstage. It was good to see them all.

On the ride home Dad told me again how proud he was of me. He was mostly proud of my heart. He said I cared for people and he admired that a lot. Even though I made mistakes, he said that I was maturing because I learned from them. Getting all A's and making the principal's list in school also made him proud.

When we pulled in our driveway, I realized my special night with my father was coming to an end, but I didn't want it to. I leaned over and gave him a big hug, knowing that we had just grown closer.

❁

This summer was just getting better and better. The next week my family was headed to Hilton Head, South Carolina. The island was such a pretty place. We flew to Savannah, Georgia, rented a car, and drove about forty miles onto the small island.

"Are we there yet?" Cassie asked as we passed the outlet stores. "It says Hilton Head but I don't see the water."

"Girl, relax," my dad said. "You asked us that from the house to the airport, and on the plane to in the car. Yes, this is Hilton Head Island. We gotta cross over the bridge, pass the excavation point, pay the toll, and we're there."

"Cassie, sweetie, we're almost at our villa," my mom said, pointing at the water on both sides of the car.

It was so blue, so pretty; I couldn't wait to go swimming in it. I was so thankful for family time. Nothing was going to make this vacation bad. My mom was always right. Five minutes later, we were parking the car to get the keys for our place.

We were here for the Week of Champions, a sports camp. It was a Christian camp my father came to every year. Sometimes we came with him. Last year we were getting ready to move, so we stayed home with my mom. This summer we were excited to come. Though the camp included different sports all week, my dad and his former pro-athlete friends were coaching the football part. That was only for two days in the mornings, so my dad would have all afternoon and the rest of the week to hang out with us. There was also basketball, baseball, tennis, soccer, and golf. Former collegiate cheerleaders coached cheerleading, Cassie's favorite pastime. The other instructors were all former pro athletes. They brought their families as well. The underprivileged kids on the island attended the free clinics.

When we got to the gorgeous, two-story villa that sat off the lake, our mouths hung open. Even my mom was impressed. And she had been a lot of places, so it took a lot to impress her.

"Charles, this place is beautiful," she said stepping inside onto a spiral staircase. The marble floors beneath my feet glistened. The paper my dad held said there were three bedrooms upstairs, and the main bedroom was on the first floor, which we knew our parents would occupy.

Clay, Cassie, and I looked at each other; we put our stuff down and raced each other up the stairs, trying to claim our space. "You guys be careful," my dad shouted.

One bedroom was larger than the others were. All

three bedrooms upstairs had their own baths, so Cassie and I didn't have to share just because we were girls. Clay couldn't even pull that one on us, so I didn't even want him to try.

"I think I should get the biggest room because I'm the oldest," he said lamely instead.

Cassie yelled, "I never get the special place; I should get it!"

"Well, I was in here first," I told the both of them. "And I'm not going anywhere."

The three of us started yelling and bickering back and forth about who was going to stay in the spacious room fit for royalty. Before we knew it, our parents were standing in the doorway, threatening to make us all sleep on the floor. I hated we'd gotten loud enough to get ourselves into trouble.

"I mean, this is just ridiculous, you guys," my dad stepped in the room and said. "This place is beautiful. Who cares if the room is big or small or whatever? You're someplace different. Each of you will have your own room and bathroom. We're here at a Christian camp, to promote sports, which emphasizes teamwork. We're here to witness to people who don't even know God. How can we do that when *we* can't even get along?"

None of us could even look at my father. He was right. We all felt bad about it. I could tell because Clay held his head low and Cassie's eyes started watering. I knew I felt bad the minute he entered the room. But my

dad didn't let up. He wanted us to understand how un-
acceptable our behavior was.

My dad continued, "So how am I supposed to go out
there and tell other kids about God if my own kids act
ungrateful? We could have been camping in the wilder-
ness in a small tent with no space, and the three of y'all
are up here arguing about who gets the biggest room."

I walked toward the doorway but my mom would not
let me out. "Where are you going?" she asked me. "Your
father is still talking to you all."

"I'm sorry, Mom. I've just decided that Dad is right.
We were wrong. I'm just happy to be here in whichever
room you all say is mine. One of them can have this
room," I said, truly getting the fact that I was selfish.

Clay and Cassie looked at each other, still trying to
figure out which one of them was going to have it. The
stares they gave each other were pretty tough looks. My
dad wasn't pleased with what he saw.

My dad surprised me and said, "That settles it. Carmen,
you get the room. The two of y'all get out of here and go
into one of the others."

"Why, Daddy?" Cassie whined.

"First of all, because I said so, and, second, because
your sister is ready to give it up. She understood the
point that I was making. It's not about having your way
all the time, guys; it's about giving of yourselves so somebody else can get a blessing. Being selfless is a bigger
blessing than getting what you want," my dad said before

coming over and hugging me after my siblings and Mom left the room. "I'm proud of you, girl."

I smiled. "I'm still bummed with myself for being bossy. I'm trying to learn how to not be like that. I don't deserve this nice room either, Dad."

Messing up my hair, he joked. "The room thing is settled. Don't be so hard on yourself."

The rest of our time in Hilton Head was so much fun. We had no more arguments. We even learned how to play golf on the gorgeous greens near our place. We shopped at the outlet stores and ate all the ice cream in the world. We went to the beach a couple of times. We went crabbing and ate the best seafood. During the camp, fifty-five kids gave their lives to Christ. My parents kept saying how amazing that was. That really made me think about my relationship with God. Am I as serious about God as I should be?

We just hated when it was time to go back home; nobody asked, "Are we there yet?" Not even Cassie. We just wished we had more time on the island. Cassie, Clay, and I went to Hilton Head thinking selfishly but left there thinking about each other. We really bonded on the island. It was a super vacation.

✪

I didn't think anything could top my outing with my dad, but then the family vacation came along and bumped that out of first place for my summer fun. But when my parents dropped us off in Durham at my auntie Chris and uncle Mark's home, there was a limousine waiting in the driveway to take Cassie and me around town. I knew my auntie Chris had something really special planned. I felt like this trip might beat all the other stuff.

I was so glad my dad changed his mind and let us come visit even though it was just a weekend visit. He and my mom had worked it out. Boy, were my parents da bomb.

"Auntie Chris, you're just the best," I said as I stretched out on the seat in front of the TV.

"What's this button for? What's that button for? What's this do?" Cassie asked quickly, not giving Auntie Chris a chance to respond as my little sister was overwhelmed with the fancy car.

"They all do something, girl. Just sit back and enjoy the ride," she told my sister. "You know I had to do something special for my little ladies. We've only got a few days together, and then your parents will be back from the coaches' retreat."

My dad was hosting a bonding thing for his coaching staff. They went to the Blue Ridge Mountains, in another part of North Carolina.

"Carmen, we should go to Grandma Annabelle's house and let Clay come out and see this," Cassie said.

Her eyes widened with more excitement than when she got a new toy. Though Clay and I had been getting along better lately, I was still happy to have a little break from him. He was pumped that my grandpa was taking him fishing.

I quickly said, "Uh, we won't bug them. We're hanging out with Auntie. Auntie, where are we going?"

"Well, we've got the limo all day. Where would you like to go?" she asked us. She explained that a good friend of hers owned the limo and was giving her a great deal on the price.

Of course, the first stop was the mall. She bought us new outfits. Mine was so flashy. She hooked Cassie and me up. My auntie got an outfit for herself too. She always wore the cutest clothes. Then we went to get our nails and toes done. Auntie wouldn't let us get red, hot polish because she knew my mom wouldn't approve. But we got a cute, peachy color. When we left the nail place, I felt like a queen. Next we went to a matinee. Movies were my favorite pasttime, and being in a cool theater that also served food was neat. The seats were so large that Cassie and I both could sit in the same chair, but we didn't have to.

My aunt was doing this first-class all the way. She was spoiling us and we loved every minute of it.

"Where is Uncle Mark?" my sister asked as we were on our way back home.

My aunt looked out the tinted window and remained quiet. *What's that about?* I wondered.

"Hello?" Cassie said in an annoying way, moving from one side of the limo to the other, trying to get my aunt to see her. "Auntie?"

"Oh, I'm sorry, baby," she said, giving my little sister a hug. "What did you ask me?"

"Uncle Mark, where is he? We've been gone all day and we haven't seen him. Where is he going to take us?"

"Cassie," I said, nudging her in the side, "you don't ask that."

"It's okay, Carmen. Your sister can ask me whatever she wants, but your uncle and I . . . I don't know. I'm sure he will do something special for you. Right now, I don't want to focus on any of that. I'm just excited to have you girls here."

"Is everything okay?" I asked, sensing she was sad.

"Never mind any of that," she said holding up both of her arms for me to nestle under one and Cassie under the other. "My two favorite little ladies in the world are here. Life is good, and nothing or nobody is going to spoil this. We're going to have a nice time."

5
Yucky Situation

A limousine? You spendin' all your money on those girls?" My uncle Mark shouted at the top of his voice, waking me from my sweet slumber. I heard my auntie say, "You're gonna wake them!"

"They need to be up!" he screamed. "They need to know how their aunt is wasting money. Somebody needs to help keep you in check. We can't afford to spend all our money on frivolous things to the point where we can't even pay our mortgage. I hope they hear me!"

"Mark, Karen gave me a deal on the limo. It wasn't full price!"

"Chris, it doesn't matter; we still can't afford to do that. We have a car that you could have very easily driven them in. That's just wasteful!"

When my uncle Mark's mean voice woke me up, I was too afraid to close my eyes again. *What is going on with my auntie?* Maybe she shouldn't have treated us to so much. *Did we get her in trouble by making her spend too much money? Is he right?* Because of us they might not be able to pay for the house stuff.

"Oh, my goodness!" I said out loud, putting my head under the pillow.

"Okay, if you're not gon' calm down," Auntie Chris shouted back in a fiery tone, "you surely gon' get your hand up out of my face!"

I was trembling then. All I could think about was my neighbor being rushed to the hospital because of domestic violence. I certainly didn't want to be in a house where it was taking place. *But what in the world can I do? Should I call 9-1-1?*

My sister was a hard sleeper, so even as the shouting grew louder, it still didn't wake up Cassie, and I was sort of glad. I didn't want both of us worrying about Aunt Chris's safety. At first, I paced back and forth, trying to figure out a plan. I had to talk to my uncle. Yeah, that was it. I had to make him see he couldn't talk to her like that. He needed to just lower his tone. I would make sure she wouldn't spend any more money on us. I had to talk to him. And if he wouldn't listen to her, maybe he would listen to me.

Then I realized that was a stupid plan. How could I

get in adults' business? He wouldn't listen to a child about stuff this important. The counselor who visited my school said we should not try to interfere in a situation like this. My aunt wouldn't want me to interfere. She'd want me to stay out of it. But I couldn't just leave this alone.

So I dropped to my knees and prayed. I needed the Lord to help me figure the whole thing out. I didn't know how. I didn't know what. But I knew He was capable.

Father, I prayed. *I hear arguing going on in the next room, and it's really, really scaring me. I know I'm just a kid and I'm not supposed to know too much, but I know those voices. They're not voices of two people who are happy with each other. Help my auntie Chris and uncle Mark. Help them not get so mad. And help my sister and I say the right things while we're in their house and do the right things so we won't make Uncle Mark angry. This is supposed to be a fun time, a good time. Please help us. In Jesus' name, amen.*

"What are you praying about this late?" Cassie said, waking up. As she stretched, my uncle's loud voice startled her. "What's that? What's he screaming about?" She jumped out of bed and sat on the floor next to where I was kneeling. "Why is he yelling at her like that, Carmen? What's going on?"

"Get back in the bed and go to sleep." I tried to ease her mind, knowing that didn't work for me.

"How can anybody go to sleep with yelling all around us? We gotta do something. We gotta go in and make sure she's all right. That's our auntie! Come on, Carmen," my little sister said as she tugged on me.

"We can't go in there," I told her, trying to pull her back.

"Yes, we can," she said, yanking me forward.

My aunt and uncle's bedroom door was cracked. We both peeked in, knowing it wasn't the right thing to do, but we didn't have the guts to go in after all. He was pointing in her face. She had tears in her eyes.

Angrily he shouted, "You can't waste our money! That's why I didn't want the girls to come here in the first place. I don't know why you feel like you have to impress or make people think we're doin' so well."

"Mark, get back!" she screamed and then pushed him onto the bed before quickly dashing out of the room in front of us.

"Auntie Chris, Auntie Chris, wait!" Cassie said, running down the hall after my aunt. My uncle heard her voice. He quickly came out into the hall and we locked eyes. His were so red and full of anger. My knees shook with fear.

"Were y'all out here in the hall listening to our conversation, Carmen?" he demanded.

I wanted so desperately to say no, because that seemed like a better answer than the truth. But I couldn't lie. Something inside my spirit wouldn't let me lie. But my mouth was shut tight. The only thing I could do was nod my head real slow.

"Look, I'm sorry you had to hear all that. But that's between me and your aunt. I don't want y'all to think that I really don't want you guys here or anything like that."

Again my head automatically nodded up and down. But at that time I didn't understand. However, what else could I say? I couldn't let him know how horrible I thought his actions were. I didn't have the guts.

"Your aunt and I don't have a lot of money right now. We can barely pay all of the bills. I know you can't understand all of this."

He said in a calmer voice, "You'll understand when you're older and making your own money and you've got bills to pay that you have to manage the money you earn. If you don't manage it well, you can be put out in the street. I know your aunt loves you guys, but I just can't allow her to blow all of our money."

"I understand and I'm sorry. I'll make sure she doesn't buy us anything else all this year. I just don't want to see you guys arguing anymore," I said, dropping my head, hoping he'd take my last statement well.

"I'll try not to fuss with her," he said as he patted me on the head.

He grabbed his keys and told me to tell my aunt he'd be back. Then he left me standing in the hallway. I couldn't move my body. The whole ordeal made my heart race so fast that I could've been in a speed race. Taking deep breaths, I sighed. *Lord, You've gotta fix them.* As I walked back to the room Cassie and I were staying in, I only hoped that God heard me and that He'd answer my request.

❂

The next day my uncle hadn't returned. I hadn't seen him since the day before, when he'd left and gave me the message to give to my auntie Chris. Actually, having him gone for most of the day was fine. She stayed strong and stopped crying. Even though we weren't out and about spending money, we still had a good time with her. We baked chocolate chip cookies and popped popcorn.

I asked my aunt if I could call my friend. I was so happy she had a calling plan where long-distance calls were cheap. She told me she had some kind of flat rate, which meant it didn't matter how long I talked or where I called in the United States; her bill was going to be the same. I had to make sure my talking wouldn't make her spend money on me unnecessarily.

My time with my aunt had been so bumpy that I needed to hear from my girlfriends. I just knew Layah and Riana were having the time of their lives, and just hearing a little bit about their fun would probably cheer me up. I was excited that this summer was a good one. I had gotten a couple of letters here and there from them before I came down to North Carolina. They put telephone numbers on all of them. It was good to get their postcards. It was good to know they missed me. Now we could chitchat. Hopefully they would be home.

Ten minutes later, I was all smiles when I successfully connected the three of us on three-way. But my smile quickly turned to a frown as I learned my buddies had problems going on as well.

Layah said, "Nope, my summer is not going that well either. You guys, I'm so glad to talk to y'all. I just found out the worst news ever."

I braced myself. What was my tough friend going to tell me? She was with her grandmother in Mississippi. Things should be fine.

"What, what?" I yelled, unable to wait.

"What's going on?" Riana asked anxiously.

"Guys, you gotta pray for my grandmother. I just found out that she's got breast cancer."

I had heard of breast cancer, but I really didn't know what it was. I was too embarrassed to tell my friend that I didn't know. Plus, I didn't want to ask too many questions. I felt if she wanted to go into more details, she would on her own. So basically I just listened.

"My dad knew before I got up here; that's why he wanted me to spend this summer with her. She's gotta have an operation and some radiation stuff. They say that with the cancer she has, she could get really sick. It's pretty bad," Layah uttered in a sad tone.

"Your grandmother's gonna be okay," I chimed in to cheer up my friend. "Let's all pray for her now."

We took a few minutes and talked to God about her

grandmother. I felt bad for my friend. If anything like that was to happen to one of my grandmothers, I didn't know what I'd do.

Riana spoke up next to tell her bummed-out story. "I was in another car accident. I was with my sixteen-year-old cousin and a car hit us. We're cool, but I had to get stitches. My whole body hurts. My cousin just got her license and her parents told us not to go anywhere. We didn't listen and we paid the consequences. I've got a big gash on my face y'all! I'm so ugly!"

Both Layah and I tried telling her she was far from ugly. It wasn't working. She wanted to have a pity party. Eventually we gave up trying and let her sulk.

Then my friends asked me how my summer was going. I didn't wanna tell them the bad stuff. We had already talked about enough. I told them about the fun I had on the date with my dad and about the great time my family had at the beach. But they knew something else was going on.

"Are you telling us everything?" Riana asked.

"Girl, somethin' ain't right with you," Layah said.

I blurted out, "Nothing, just . . . sad."

"What do you mean, you're sad? You gotta tell us more than that," Riana said.

"You know we care."

I broke down and said with a heavy heart, "My auntie Chris and her husband are fussing a lot, almost fighting. I wanna go home, but I can't get my parents because they're up in the mountains. They won't be here until tomorrow."

"Oh no," Riana said.

"Stay out of his way," Layah told me. "You and your sister just need to be extra nice."

"Girl, I'm trying to do that, but I'm also worried about my aunt, you know? He doesn't seem like a good husband. He's been so mean to her," I told them.

My aunt opened the door and said, "Carmen, the cookies are ready! Hot and fresh! We're having a ball here. Hurry up and get off the phone, honey, okay?"

"Okay, Auntie Chris."

"Did she say y'all are having a ball?" Layah asked. "She must not know you want to go home."

"I gotta go, but let's keep praying for each other. Soon, soon, soon we'll all be home again. I'm looking forward to middle school."

"Yeah, me too," Layah said. "And I wasn't at first."

"I hope my face heals before it's time to start school," Riana said.

"Girl, it will," Layah said before we hung up the phone.

Just before going into the kitchen, I studied my aunt for a second. She had some kind of peace that was amazing to see. She was singing to herself. She had a smile on her face. She and my sister were having a ball. She wasn't letting anything get her down. I liked that about her. In the midst of her going through trouble, she was happy. I would have to remember that.

✪

It was the last full day we would be there. We still hadn't seen my uncle. Cassie asked my aunt why he hadn't been home. She didn't tell us, so I tried not to think about it.

Auntie Chris came into the room and said, "I have so many wonderful plans. You guys hurry up. We've gotta leave. We've got a big day."

I ran up to the door and said in a panic, "No, Auntie Chris! No way! You are not doing anything extra special for us. You're not spending any money."

Cassie ran over and said, "Ha! Speak for yourself. You can spend money on me!" I hit her on the side. "Ouch!" my sister exclaimed.

My aunt told me, "Girl, get up and get ready. Don't worry about plans for today."

As soon as she shut the door, I reminded Cassie, "Have you seen our uncle here in the last couple of days? You heard him say he's mad because she spent money on us. But yet you don't care. You want her to get in more trouble by spending more money? Come on, Cassie! Don't be like that. We've got to convince her not to do that. And if she tries to buy us anything, we've got to tell her no. Are you listening?"

"Yeah, I hear you. I don't want there to be any more problems with them. I hated it when he got mad. But you're right."

84

In the car on our way to the mall, my sister and I went back and forth trying to convince my aunt we didn't need anything else. She turned up the music in the car louder, letting us know that she wasn't trying to hear what we had to say.

"Let's dance, girls," she said cheerfully to us.

What more could Cassie and I do? My aunt had her own mind. We ate lunch at Ruby Tuesdays, which was inside the mall.

She said to us, "I know you're worried about what you all witnessed between your uncle and me. I know my husband said some things. I know you haven't seen him in a couple of days. It's not because of you. He and I just need some time away. He forgot that I saved my money, some extra money that he agreed about before you guys even came. I knew long ago the budget I had saved to spend on you all. I reminded him. So relax!"

I told my auntie that I thought about calling 9-1-1 but she said that Uncle Mark wasn't violent; he was just upset about their bills. I also told her about the incident at the Thomases' home, and the hotline number that she could call to talk confidentially, if she needed to. After all of our discussion, I felt better and enjoyed my lunch.

Cassie started talking to Auntie Chris about tumbling and some of her favorite interests, and I started telling her how excited I was about going to middle school. Having her as an aunt was great. She understood. My mom was great, but Auntie Chris was cool.

When the bill came, however, all the fun stopped. My aunt gave the waiter a credit card and he came back and whispered something in her ear.

"What do you mean 'not enough funds'? What? Try this one." She sat there tapping her finger.

Moments later he came back again and said, "This didn't go through either."

"What!?" She picked up her cell phone and started dialing. "I can't believe you did this. How dare you!"

My sister and I had money that my parents had given us. I had twenty dollars. Cassie had ten.

Then I said to my aunt, "Is this enough, tip and everything?"

With her eyes watering, she stood up and said to both of us, "Thanks. Let's go."

Apparently my uncle had done something with her cards. I didn't know what was up, but it didn't seem right. *If they share the money, how could he do that?*

When we got back to my aunt's house, my aunt said before we went up to our room, "Don't worry, girls. I'll deal with this. I need to talk to him. Stay in your room this time, please."

"Auntie Chris!" I ran up to her and said. "Please, I don't want you guys fussing."

"My husband gets angry and loses his temper. That's just how he expresses himself."

"You'll be okay if he yells at you?" I asked.

"Yes."

My sister and I took a nap. However, once again the yelling woke us up.

"I work hard for my money! You're not gonna cancel my credit cards and leave me no access to any of my stuff. Are you crazy?"

Cassie hugged me. "Carmen, I'm scared."

"It's okay. Auntie Chris said so," I replied to her.

"I stopped the cards. I know you got an impulse to shop. There's no telling how much money you would've spent. I'll turn everything on once the girls are gone."

"Where is my suitcase?!" my aunt said frantically.

The next thing Cassie and I heard was the shattering of glass. She and I were terrified then. What in the world was going on in the next room? Was anybody hurt? What were we to do? This was all too much. I didn't really understand domestic violence before now, but hearing that loud noise made me understand. When people in a relationship don't get along, it can escalate to a really yucky situation.

6

Peaceful Night

"Mom, Mom, hurry! You've gotta come quick!" I said in the receiver after dialing my mom's cell phone.

In one hand I held the cordless and in the other I held my sister's hand. She was clutching my hand tightly. We were both petrified.

"Carmen, sweetie, you've gotta calm down," my mom said, not understanding the seriousness of the situation.

"You've gotta hurry. Something's wrong here. Where are y'all?" I cried.

"Baby, slow down; what's going on over there? You're not making any sense. Talk to me," she said in a rational voice.

Suddenly a door slammed, making the

bed Cassie and I were in move with vibration. "Carmen? Are you guys okay? What was that noise? I hear your sister crying. Okay, sweetie, talk to me. We were coming to get you guys later, but we can come now. We're at Dad's parents' house with Clay. We can be there shortly, but sweetie, I need to know what's going on. Talk to me."

"Mom, they're fighting," I told her, unable to stop shaking.

"Who's fighting?"

"Auntie Chris and Uncle Mark. We heard something break. We don't wanna go in there," I told her. "Mom, you've gotta come quick. We think Auntie Chris wants to leave and he won't let her, Mom."

"Okay, let's pray. Lord, right now we ask for Your protection. We ask You to bring peace to Mark and Chris's home. Let love and understanding flow abundantly. Give my daughters peace and keep them in Your loving care. In Jesus' name. Amen. We're on the way. Carmen, you guys will be okay 'til we get there," my mom said, trying to reassure herself, with something I couldn't confirm.

So then I said, "I–I–I don't know, Mom."

The next voice I heard was that of my dad's. "Carmen, we'll be there in a minute. Hold it together for your little sister. You stay strong so you don't scare her, okay, big girl?"

"Okay, I will, Dad. It reminds me of the time . . . ," I said, thinking of the Thomas family.

"No, it's okay. It won't get like that. Just calm down. We'll be there in a second."

I told Cassie that Mom and Dad were on the way. I felt better knowing we were going to get our auntie some help.

"Oh, you think you're going somewhere?" we heard my uncle scream at my aunt.

She said loudly, "Get out of my way, Mark! Get out of my way! I'm sure you've scared the girls! I need to check on them!"

"You're worrying about the wrong thing," he told her.

"I know you're scaring them. Move!"

Cassie got up, ran out of the bedroom, and went to my aunt's door. She scurried so fast; I didn't have time to react. I would've held her back. She didn't need to go in there. I didn't need to go in there either, but I couldn't let my little sister go alone. My dad told me to set an example and to watch out for her. How could I do that if I was scared in the guest room? So I fled behind her just in time to see her kick my uncle in the back of his leg, making him buckle down and shout out, "Ouch!"

When he moved to the side a little, both Cassie and I ran up toward our aunt. However, before we got there, my sister leaned down and grabbed her right foot. Blood was streaming from it, as if it were a river. When I looked down, I saw glass from one of Auntie Chris's vases covering the floor.

"Will you leave now?" she shouted to her husband as she rushed over to my sister. "Carmen, go in my bathroom, baby, and get a towel quickly—girl, go!"

"It's a piece of glass stuck in it!" Cassie said as she fell to the floor.

I couldn't move fast enough. The evening was bad. Add my sister getting hurt on top of everything else and I could barely take it.

"Carmen, come on, honey!" my aunt called out to me.

"I'll go check and see what's taking her so long," I heard my uncle say.

"No, please, Mark. Can't you see? Go!" she pleaded with him.

I finally rushed out of the bathroom and saw him with his arms folded, looking down at my aunt and sister. He wouldn't leave, though. Boy, did I want him to.

My aunt took my sister's foot and tried to take out the big piece of glass. My sister cried, "No!"

"Come on, Cassie, calm down," Auntie Chris said. "You've gotta let me try to get this out, baby. I need to see how deep it is. You might have to get stitches."

Cassie moaned, "Stitches? Oh no!"

I don't know why my aunt said that. That made my sister jump up and hobble all around. I was so happy my aunt's room had hardwood floors because my sister was leaving a blood trail. Though I wasn't sure it'd come out, I knew it wouldn't have if it was carpet because at our old house the carpet had tough stains that took three shampoos to finally come out. We didn't need anything else for my uncle to be mad about. But before anybody could say anything else in the house, the doorbell rang.

"It's my parents! It's my parents!" Cassie cried as she hobbled out into the hallway.

In a terrified voice, my aunt said, "You called your parents? Oh, this is just great. Your parents are never gonna let y'all come again."

As she went down the hall to answer the door, Uncle Mark said, "After all this, you're still worried about whether or not the girls can visit, Chris? We've got a major marriage problem and you're worried about your sister getting mad and not letting the girls come back again. How about I might not let them come back again?"

"How about I won't be married to you anymore?" she turned around and screamed at him.

I ran around her and opened up the front door. I'd never been so happy to see my parents in all my life. I clung to my mother with a hug so tight.

The next few hours were such a blur. My mom doctored my sister and found that her cut was not serious. My dad took my aunt and uncle to the other side of the house and had a talk with them.

"Everything is okay now," my mom said as she helped us finish packing our suitcases.

"I know he doesn't like us, Mom," Cassie said.

"I believe he does. He's probably angry about some other stuff, but it's easy for him to mention you two as the problem."

"Is she gonna be okay? Is she gonna stay with him?" my sister asked.

"Tonight we're gonna take her back with us. I can't answer what's next for them. But I can tell you right now we can pray."

I agreed. "Okay, Mom. Let's do that."

Cassie and I held hands with my mom. The prayer she said to God comforted us. We couldn't have worked this out for my aunt. We just had to place it all in God's hands. In silence, the five of us drove back to my dad's parents' house to pick up Clay and head back home. I was safe, and at peace.

✪

A couple of days later, I woke up in the bed again with my sister. Though she and I had bonded a bit, I was sort of tired of her feet in my mouth! She slept so wild. But when I came to, I realized I didn't care. I could put up with the inconvenience because my aunt was spending a couple of weeks with us.

"This is gonna be such a great day!" Cassie said as she yawned and stretched.

"Cassie, what are you talking about?" I asked.

She said, "It's the Fourth of July!"

Cassie then made a clean break toward the kitchen. I knew my sister loved cheerleading, tumbling, gymnastics, and all that, but she needed to run track. The girl was way too fast. One minute she was here and the next minute she was there.

Clay and I hadn't spent much time together since we were in different places over the past week. And since he'd been home, he'd been in football camp. I didn't realize I'd missed him so much. When he came to my room and asked me if I wanted to play Xbox, I jumped to the challenge. I probably couldn't beat my brother on the machine, but I was excited that I could spend time with him.

"So what you been up to, Sis? What's been going on?" he asked me, sort of weirding me out.

He never really cared about how I was. *Had he missed me too? Wow!*

I hugged him really hard and pushed him off the side of the coffee table. "Aww! You care about me!"

"Yeah, a little. You just scored on me easy," he said as he jumped back into the game we were playing.

I didn't know how to really work the stick for basketball. I'd turn it one way and my player would go another. Somehow I ended up doing something major that made my brother think I had mad skills. He even tried teaching me ways of improving my game—that game made me realize that maybe he did miss me more than a little.

"Nothing's been going on with me, Clay. I'm just happy to be home and have Auntie Chris with us."

"Yeah, I heard about all that."

"How was football practice for you?"

"It's growing on me. I'm a quarterback and my arm is pretty strong. I'll probably start next year. Gotta keep my grades up and learn the plays."

"Cool, Clay!"

The phone rang and my brother tried to grab it. I must've been faster than I thought, because when I saw how bad he wanted to get it, I went for it too.

"Hello?" I said, wanting to know who it was.

"Oh, this is Hayli and Haven. Can we speak to Clay? Is he in?" a girl asked as the other girl giggled.

"He's right here," I said, being very silly.

My brother yanked the phone from me.

"Girls, oooh!"

My brother spoke to them for less than two minutes. They got off quick. I drilled him with all sorts of questions. He ignored me, saying he didn't have time for girls. I was excited. I guess it sort of made me proud that my brother was getting popular. And just in time too. Because I'd be going to middle school next year and it'd be so cool to have a popular brother.

Right before we were leaving for the fireworks, we went to an outdoor church service. The dark blue sky was so beautiful with all the stars. I just gazed while the choir sang. It sounded like the angels were singing. And when my pastor got up to speak, I couldn't help but keep my full attention on every word he was saying. It was like he was talking directly to me.

"Yeah, this night is supposed to be about the fireworks. It's Independence Day for our country and I like to see the sparks fly too. I like to see the bright lights in the sky. I love America," Pastor Wright said to the audience. "But tonight I wanna talk to the saints about letting your sparks fly for Jesus."

He went on to say that it's not enough just to pray to God. It's not enough just to believe, but it has to be a daily surrendering of our thoughts and our actions to God. For those of us who hadn't accepted God, we needed to personally give our lives to Jesus now. We needed to realize that we were sinners, believe that Jesus Christ died for our sins, and confess our sins and then we would be saved.

Then I realized, for sure he was talking to me. Though I believed by faith that God was up in heaven, I had never said that I wanted Christ to be the Lord of my life. I wanted fireworks in my heart to blast for Him. I realized sitting in my seat that I was ready to take my relationship with the Lord to the next level. I wanted to walk down the aisle and make this official.

Pastor Wright continued, "Life isn't always easy. Even being a Christian doesn't mean you're perfect. But you cannot make it without Him and you can't make it to heaven if you haven't accepted Him."

Then and there in my seat, a chill went up my spine. Going to heaven was the only option for me. The only alternative was a fiery place and I didn't wanna spend eternity there. I had to do what the Bible required to make sure I was saved.

"So much stuff is happening now in the world. Husbands abusing their wives, drunk drivers killing teenagers in cars, and diseases of all kinds in our land. We never know when our last day will be. We might not have the chance again to let God in our lives. I urge you all to let your soul soar to the sky like this," my pastor said as he set off a firecracker.

Red lights, green lights, and white ones went up into the sky. Boy, it was a marvelous sight.

He continued, "God loves you. The beautiful lights in the sky will be the way you feel inside when the Holy Spirit dwells in you. There will be some tough days ahead, but with God on your side, you can't lose."

The pastor then prayed and extended an invitation for people to come to the altar and give their lives to Christ. My heart was for it, but my feet stayed still.

What are you doing, Carmen Brown? I thought to my-self. *Go down there! Say yes to Jesus!* But I didn't move. I don't know why I didn't move, but I didn't move. I wanted to be down there. Unable to move, I shed a tear.

❂

Later that night after ice cream, more fireworks, and time with my aunt, I went to bed. My sister was knocked out. I, on the other hand, was softly crying into the pillow. I didn't even realize my mother had walked in. She sat on the bed and rubbed my head.

"Carmen, sweetie, what's wrong?"

I sat up and hugged her so tight. "Mom, I wanted to give my life to Christ today and I didn't. I couldn't go down there. I don't know what's wrong with me. What if I don't get another chance?"

"Sweetheart, I've always known you've had a special place in your heart for God. You may not have verbally said that He was your Lord and Savior, but your heart has shown you love Him. If you want to, you can pray the prayer of salvation right now."

"And I'll be saved?" I asked with excitement, looking into her eyes with the help of moonlight from the window.

"Yes, you will be saved."

"I'll go to heaven?" I asked.

"Yup. You'll go to heaven if you truly believe what you've said and prayed. Like the pastor said tonight, the Christian life won't be easy, but it's the best one we could have. In the Bible there's a book called John. . . ."

"Yeah, that's one of the four Gospels."

My mom smiled. "Good! Someone's been doing a good job in Sunday school. Well, John 3:16 says what? 'For God so loved the world, that he gave his only begotten Son, that whosoever believeth in him should not perish, but have everlasting life.' Do you believe that, Carmen?"

"Yes, Mom," I said, glad for my answer.

"Close your eyes and talk to Him. Ask Jesus to come into your heart then, Ladybug."

"Lord," I prayed, holding my mom's hand real tight, "this is Carmen Browne, the girl who talks to You all the

time. I know You can hear me. And I think I've been doing it right. Now I want You to please come into my heart.
I wanna go to heaven one day and be with You and the
Father and my mom's father. I love You, Jesus, and I believe that You died for my sins." My mom squeezed my
hand even tighter, I'm sure, remembering her dad in a
special way. "So I'm asking You right now to forgive me of
all the things I've done wrong and help me to be better. In
Jesus' name, amen."

"Awesome, sweetie," my mom said as she wiped tears
from her eyes. "You are now a believer."

"So now I need to walk down the aisle at church and
stuff?"

"Yeah, you can. But you're saved now. Walking down the
aisle will get you a membership in church and baptized."

"Mom, thanks."

"The Holy Spirit told me to come in here and check
on you."

"How will I know when the Holy Spirit is talking to
me?" I asked.

"Just know that the Holy Spirit is a part of the Trinity.
The Holy Spirit leads you to do the right things, not the
wrong ones. You've got to pray daily and listen to Him, so
that when He speaks you'll recognize His voice."

"Oh, wow," I said, feeling great about what I'd just
done.

My mother and I talked for a few more minutes,
and she began telling me that she'd help me grow as a

Christian. She also said that my friends and even difficult situations that I faced would help my growth. And although physically I didn't feel any different like some other presence was inside of me or whatever, I did feel strong. I did feel excited. I did feel so glad because I knew that one day I'd be in heaven. One day I'd sing with the angels. One day I would be perfect. One day Jesus would let me in, because I'd let Him in.

My mother kissed me on the cheek, told me how proud of me she was, and shut the door. I walked over to the window and looked at the pretty sky. It was a gorgeous summer night. Fireworks were still going off in different places. But even with loud noises all around, I wasn't disturbed. I took comfort in knowing I was saved. I had such a peaceful night.

Chaos Everywhere

It was mid-July and I missed my girl-friends Layah and Riana. The three of us hadn't been together in a long time, so when Layah invited Riana and me to come to her family reunion barbecue at her house, I was excited. Layah spent part of the summer at her grandma's house. Instead of her spending the whole summer at her grandma's house, Mr. Golf decided to bring her grandma to their house to spend some time.

That excitement quickly dwindled when we first arrived at the Golfs' home. Riana and I were supposed to be there at 11:00. We arrived about 11:40. My dad took us, but just as we were leaving the house, I got a call from Riana asking if she could ride with us.

Stopping by to get her and my father swinging by his office and staying longer than we'd planned ended up making us late.

Riana and I were patient, though. I mean, what could we do? He was our ride. She and I just caught up on what had happened to her over the summer. I was relieved to see that she was better from the car accident she was in.

When Layah opened the door, she didn't even say hello. She just turned around and walked back into her house. She was so rude.

Quickly I said, "Oh, so you're not gonna speak?"

"I was expecting you guys a long time ago," Layah finally turned around and said to us.

"We're not even an hour late," I told her.

Riana explained, "Layah, Carmen's dad had to take care of something. We couldn't help it."

"Well, you could've called me," Layah huffed.

"Call from what? I don't have a cell phone. And what's the big deal anyway? You've got all these people in your house, all this family. I didn't think it was a big deal," I said honestly.

Layah scoffed. "I was depending on you two to help me and my dad get things ready."

"Well, you didn't tell us that. I might as well just try to stop my dad now before he leaves. I'll leave with him," I said, trying to flag my dad down.

"Carmen, if that's what you want to do, then fine," she said in a mean tone.

Before I could show her that I wasn't playing, I saw my father pull away. It was too late. I was stuck.

"I guess I have to stay here," I said, sort of in a not-so-nice way.

"No, you don't have to stay here. You can walk home," Layah said.

Riana came between us and put her arms around the two of us. "Oh, come on. We're just seeing each other. We haven't been together in a long time. We're the three musketeers, the three peas in a pod. We're like the three little pigs, but our house isn't built out of straw; it's built of bricks. Come on, guys, we're best friends. Let's act like it."

"I'm not calming down, Riana. Carmen always thinks the party stops and ends with her," Layah said, kicking the door shut with her heel after Riana and I went in.

I didn't want to have a big confrontation with Layah. This was her event. Her family was here. This was supposed to be a good time. It had been a long time since we hung out. We weren't supposed to have turmoil. However, Layah had it wrong. She was the one who liked to have things her way.

I didn't back down but retorted, "Look, Layah, you don't have to have an attitude. If you want an apology because my dad made us late, then fine. I'm sorry. But I do care about you and I am excited to be here. You don't have to say I want my way all the time because I don't feel that way at all. What's really wrong with you anyway?" I asked.

My friend fell down to the steps and let out a sob. "My dad's mad at me because I didn't set the table. But I was waiting to set all the silverware and everything out when you guys got here, but y'all never came. And then he yelled at me in front of the family. My grandmother's here, but she can't really do anything because she's so sick. She's gonna be living with us, and I don't like to see her so weak and frail looking. It's just hard being me right now. I'm not supposed to be mad at you guys. I just can't take this. It's too hard."

Both Riana and I sat down on the opposite sides of Layah and became teary eyed. I didn't know what was going through Riana's mind. She actually didn't say too much. I could only imagine that she was just grateful that the car accident wasn't worse. In my mind, I kept hearing the shatter of glass at my aunt's home. Life was hard; life was tough. But deep inside I believed there was a God out there. There was a Jesus who lived, hung on the cross, and died but rose again so that we would have hope. I believed as long as I gave all my problems to God I would be at peace.

Then I thought back to when I first arrived at Layah's house. I realized I didn't need to act so harshly just because she acted mean. I should've asked my friend if she was okay. I should've been more sensitive. I started beating myself up wondering why I didn't react more like Jesus would to my friend.

I'd accepted Christ only a couple of weeks earlier, but

I was still being real mean sometimes. What in the world was I all about? I was so happy when my dad finally came and got me. Riana stayed longer. Layah gave me a big hug, and we forgave one another. I told her we were cool, which was true. I was fine with her. I just wasn't fine with myself.

✪

"What do you mean, you guys are planning a pool party and this Sunday is my birthday?" I said with disgust as I entered the family room and heard my brother and sister scheming to crash my big day.

"What's the big deal, Sis?" Clay said to me. "It worked really good last year. We need a summer party. We want our friends over too."

"Yeah," Cassie chimed in. "It's not like Mom and Dad are gonna let us have a whole bunch of parties or whatever. We gotta share this one with you."

I said defiantly, "No, no. You guys have this all wrong. That was last year. We had to do it that way because we were about to move."

I didn't want to be the one spoiling all of their fun before it even began, but I had to be real. I had to be honest. I had to tell them what was really going on inside of me. I did not want to share my party with them again. Yeah, it worked out last year, but I had no choice. We were moving. This was a new time—my time.

My siblings could have another little fun thing with their own friends on their own time. They couldn't mess up my day. Not anymore, no. I wasn't going for it.

"I don't care what you guys say," I said to them, putting my hands up in both of their faces. "The answer is no."

"Well, you don't get to be the decision maker," Clay told me.

He pushed my hand away. "Don't push me like that, Clay!"

"I didn't push you. I just moved your hand out of my face," he quickly told me.

Walking over to the other side of the room with my arms folded, I was hot! *Why do I have to share?* On their birthdays they never let me have friends over.

"Mom has already said we could do it. You're just selfish," Cassie teased.

"That's not fair!" I turned around and said to them both. "Did you guys even ask Mom and Dad to have your own thing? This is my birthday! If you give me any present at all, I want it to be for my birthday party to be with my friends alone. You guys can come because we're related, but it's not fair that your friends get to come too."

"Your little party wouldn't be anything without my crew anyway," Clay said mockingly, referring to his friends.

I picked up the plastic cup that one of them had just finished drinking out of and whirled it at him so hard that he couldn't duck fast enough.

"Why are you being such a brat?" he asked, holding his brow where the cup hit.

"Because I want to have fun with my friends, you're calling me a brat?" I said.

"Carmen, it's always your way or no way," he lashed out.

I thought about what he was saying and I didn't agree with it at all. I had compromised so many times when it came to Clay and Cassie. I'd gotten in trouble for Clay a few months ago. I disobeyed what my parents said to help him search for his birth parents. How dare he even give me drama. And my sister—I protected her at my aunt's house. I tried to be the big one, the big sister, but this one day—one little day—was my day, and I shouldn't have to share with either one of them. *Is that so wrong?* I asked myself.

"Fine, I'm going to tell Mom," my sister said. "She's gonna make you do it."

Before I could grab my sister and say, *Hey, let's just not worry Mom. Let's just all calm down and work this out. . . .* Cassie ran up the stairs, yelling, "Mom! Mom," in this annoying voice that made me even angrier.

"You're a trip, Carmen. You never want to share," Clay said to me before sitting in a chair and turning on the TV.

"I share just like you share the remote."

"So. Two wrongs don't make a right," he looked up at me and replied.

I said, "No, but I'm just asking for one day out of 365 of them."

Before he said anything else, my mother was coming down the stairs. Cassie was dragging her. I knew I wouldn't stand a chance.

"Cassie, honey, I'm coming," my mom said.

"Mom, tell Carmen that she can't tell us that we can't have friends over when she has her party. Tell her, Mom, tell her," Cassie said boldly.

I started going past my mother up the stairs she had just come down. My mother said something to Cassie. I'm sure she told Cassie to stay in her place and not to tell her what to say or how to handle a situation.

My mom stopped me and said, "Carmen, honey, I want to talk to you about this."

"No, Mom. Whatever. You want them to have a party with me, fine, whatever. I guess I have no choice about my own little party this year."

"Girl, get back down here now. We need to talk about this," my mom said sternly.

"I'm sorry, Mom, I can't talk about it. The decision has already been made. What's left for me to say? You're the grown-up. I'm a kid; you get to decide. I have to share my party. I got it," I said as I stormed upstairs. I couldn't even shut my door. I knew my mom would be coming inside any second to set me straight. I knew I was too big for my britches, and I thought I'd lost my mind talking to her like that. But once again I was confused at all that was going on inside me.

Why, once again, was I handling things so badly? Seeing it from my siblings' point of view, would it be so bad for them to really enjoy my party with some of their guests there as well? Would I really be leaving my special day by giving in just a little bit? My head turned to the mirror and on it was a bookmark with four letters really big: WWJD. That made me feel even worse. Even Jesus would've said I had asked Him to live inside of me. Why in the world couldn't I act more like He would?

✪

A week had passed and I was still trying to understand what this whole "Christian walk" thing really meant, ever since the night I'd looked up at the stars with my mom by my side and said, "Yes, I believe there is a God. Come into my life. Let me live forever." Things from that point on had not been so clear.

How many times a day was I supposed to talk to God? I talked to my mom and she basically told me that I could talk to God as many times as I wanted to. I could pray to Jesus anytime I felt like it. And I didn't have to really look for Him to do anything. I just needed to trust that He had my life in His hands and then I'd have peace.

But how could I have peace when stuff came up? When people made me angry and I couldn't control how I felt inside, what was I to do then? My life was supposed to be so great now since I was walking with God. However, it seemed crazier since I started walking with Him. I didn't want to have bad thoughts anymore. I didn't want to be swayed to do stuff my way. I didn't want the devil to have any chance of coming in. I was so confused and it all just made me more upset.

✪

My family was at VSU for the big football barbecue before the start of the team's summer camp next week. The players and coaches were there with their families. Some of the administration and their families were there as well.

That meant I was there and so was Spence. I hadn't seen him since the time I'd been at his house and we sort of didn't get along. I saw him from a distance tossing footballs around with my brother. I didn't know what to do. Part of me wanted to go up and say, "Hey." Then I thought, *He should say hello first.* So I did other stuff.

One hour passed and we hadn't spoken. Then another hour passed, and he still hadn't said anything. I ate and another passed. Then it was almost time to go, and Spence hadn't said hello to me yet. Boy, was I boiling like a pot on the stove turned up high! Then I finally saw him walking toward me. I actually looked over both of my shoulders to make sure I wasn't imagining his intent to chat with me. I didn't want to embarrass myself by saying hello and have him ignore me. I just stood near the goalpost.

"Hey, there you are! I've been looking for you all day," he said, sort of out of breath as he jogged the rest of the way up to me.

I couldn't believe he said he'd been looking for me. Yeah, it was a big football field with a lot of people on it, but I saw him. He was with my brother. It wasn't that hard to find me. Not knowing what to say to him, I sort of half smiled.

"What's wrong with you? I just wanted to hang out with you before it was time to go. Is that cool? I know we haven't talked since you came to my house. You left angry with me. I know you're not still mad," he said, being nice. "Come on, you wanna duke it out?"

I saw nothing funny. I looked at him with irritation all over my face. He knew I was still fuming.

"Are you gonna say anything, Carmen?" he asked.

"What is it that you want me to say, Spence? It's almost time to go. You came to me at the end of the barbecue. You said you'd looked for me, but I mean, how hard did you really look?"

"Did you see me today?" he asked.

"Yeah," I said quickly, not realizing that was a trick question.

"Well then, why didn't you come up to me?"

"I . . . I just, I just . . . ," I said, tripping over my words.

"You can't even answer it, and now you're mad at me because you're saying I came up to you too late? Oh, girl, come on. We're friends. At least I wanna be your friend, but you're making it hard. I don't understand girls. They have to make little things such a big deal." Spence threw his hands in the air.

Snake the former tough guy who had turned his life around, came up to us. I hadn't seen him in so long. He had really grown. Now I could see why my dad was excited to have him train the college football players. I sort of thought of him as my other big brother. He came over and put Spence in a headlock.

"I know you're not giving my friend Carmen a hard time now, are you, boy?" Snake asked.

"Naw, man. Come on, Snake. Let me up, let me up! She's giving me a hard time. But that's okay. You can talk to her. I'm out." Spence wiggled his way out from under Snake and dashed faster away from me than when he first came.

"Man, girl, what'd you do to your friend?" Snake probed.

Feeling bad, I said, "I don't know; it's like this whole Christian thing is really hard for me. Do you have it figured out?"

"Well, come on. Let's walk and talk because I know your dad is looking for you. Your family is ready to go."

"I know you've got a record deal, you do Christian rap, and you've got a good job. I remember back when I first moved here and you scared Clay, Cassie, and me when you were with your friends in the woods. But now you're so different." I desperately wanted to know how Snake stayed strong.

"God is what's changed me. I always had a good heart. I was messing with y'all back then, tryin' to be tough. Now I'm seeking God's heart. He directs my steps. And, Carmen, if you've given your life to Him, be happy and let Him direct you," Snake advised as we walked toward the crowd.

"But I don't know where He's taking me. I don't know why I feel so mean sometimes, or why I want to boss somebody around and have things my way," I said. "It's just so much about this whole Christian thing that I don't understand. I'm feeling like I'm messing up and I'm making even more mistakes."

We stopped at the fifty-yard line and Snake turned to me and said, "Just like you're talking to me, talk to Him. Everything that you're feeling makes perfect sense. That's okay. You're just a young believer. I had some of those questions too, but He wants you to come to Him with all of it. He'll supply the answers."

"So do you have all the answers now?" I asked the friend I could see standing before me.

"No, I'll never have all the answers, but daily God supplies me what I need to know. He can help you too. Don't stress on all this stuff. You want to do right, then do it. Walk with Him in mind all the time. And when you mess up, ask for forgiveness. This is a faith walk. Tell Him the way you feel and ask Him to help you be strong. Does that make any sense to you?"

I nodded yes.

"Talk to Him now. I'll tell your parents you'll be right over," Snake said as he headed toward my parents and left me to pray.

I began silently, *Lord, the last couple of weeks, I don't know if You've been proud of me. I've been trying to find You, but I think I've been going in the wrong direction. I get so frustrated, so mad at myself and I don't know why. But I don't understand it. I need You to help me. I believe that You can help me live the way You want me to live, talk the way You want me to talk, and think the way You want me to think. Help me, God, please. I want to be better. I'm tired of chaos everywhere.*

8

Bright Beam

The next day I woke up on Sunday morning so full of energy and excitement that I could have run a marathon and won. I looked at the Barbie clock on Cassie's dresser and saw that it was only 6:15 in the morning. I was usually the one to sleep forever, but this morning—today—something was different. Something inside of me was motivating me to walk with God.

Stretching, I tried to be quiet so I wouldn't wake my sister. I looked out the window and silently prayed, *Lord, thank You for another day. Thank You for how great I feel this morning. It's as if I woke up on the right side of the bed, and I know it's because I've given it all to You. Keep helping me, please, in Jesus' name, amen.*

I turned around and I noticed my mom smiling from the doorway. She loved me so much.

"Good morning," I said as I walked over to her.

"Good morning to you too, honey."

Her embrace felt so good. She was dressed in a jogging suit and tennis shoes. I wondered why.

"Where are you going?" I asked her.

"Right now, your aunt and I are going to walk around the block."

She must have seen the excitement in my eyes because she asked, "Do you want to come?"

"Yes," I quickly responded as I went to throw on some clothes.

The end of July in Virginia always got extremely hot. Upper nineties were normal for the afternoon, but since it was early in the morning, it was a cool seventy-two degrees. It was perfect weather for a morning stroll.

"We have to get back so I can cook breakfast before church," my mom said as she left the room.

I met Mom and Auntie Chris outside. Auntie Chris pinched my cheeks, and the three of us started walking.

"You know, I'm glad you're coming with us," Auntie Chris said to me as I stood between the two of them. "I've really enjoyed being here with you guys for this month while your uncle and I are working things out."

In my mind, Uncle Mark was the enemy. I didn't like him anymore. He had hurt her. He had hurt Cassie and me. I hoped she wasn't telling me she was going back to live with him.

"He'll be here sometime this afternoon to take me back home," she said.

"No!" I said to her, putting my body directly in front of her so that she couldn't walk any farther.

She had to hear me out. She had to listen to the voice of reason. There was no way I could allow her to make this horrible mistake. Uncle Mark was not good for her. She needed to know that I didn't want her to go back home with him.

"Okay, Auntie Chris, I know I'm just a little girl . . . ," I said, really wanting her to hear me out.

Auntie Chris cut in and said, "No, you're a young lady, about to go to middle school."

"Well, okay then, that's why you have to listen to me, because I am growing up and I know more now." My eyes started watering as I talked to my aunt.

"Honey, it's okay," my mom said as she stroked my back.

"Mom, you weren't even there when it was really bad. Auntie Chris was scared. Cassie and I were scared. He was mean. She shouldn't go back and live with him."

"You're right, it was a scary situation, Carmen. But my husband loves me and I love him, and he's been getting help for his anger. God's been working with him. He's apologized and I've forgiven him, but we're going to get some counseling together. That's a big part of why I'm going home. I also need to deal with my tendency to impulse shop and not manage our money well. Uncle Mark and I realize that with the Lord's help, together we can both be better."

Feeling sad and pitiful, I just sobbed.

Stroking my hair, my aunt just held me and said, "Oh, Carmen, you're growing into such a mature young lady. I'm so proud of you and thankful that you love me so much. What am I going to do with you?"

"Mom, you knew she was leaving?" I questioned my mother in disbelief.

"I just found out on Friday, honey. Yesterday we had the football barbecue, and, besides, Chris felt that it was best if she told you herself."

"Do you really think Uncle Mark is better now?" I asked with uncertainty.

They both nodded.

I only hoped they were telling the truth. I only wanted my aunt to be happy. If my uncle was who she wanted and he would treat her like she deserved to be treated, then I guess I was all for it.

"Okay, well, I'm going to miss you."

"I will be here most of the day and then you'll come and see me soon."

"Uh, no. I don't think I'm ever coming to see you again," I told her.

We all laughed.

Minutes later we were marching and singing. My

mom and her sister sang some old song, "Guide My Feet, Lord." I remembered hearing it, but I didn't know the words. However, by the time we came halfway down our trail, I was singing with them. "Guide my feet, Lord, while I run this race. Guide my feet, Lord, while I run this race. Guide my feet, Lord, while I run this race because I don't want to run this race in vain."

It meant so much to me at that moment. It was sort of what I had said yesterday on the football field talking to God. I needed Him to tell me the way to go, or show me the way to go. I wanted Him to help me not go my own way. I needed Him to help me trust Him. I needed Him to help me have joy and peace. He must have heard me because today I woke up with a smile on my face. God is good, and I sang that song over and over again with them with a whole lot of feeling.

We stopped when we got to the Thomases' home. There was a big For Sale sign in the yard, and Michael and his mom were putting boxes in a U-Haul. It was so good to see Mrs. Thomas. We'd prayed for the Thomas family.

"Mom, can I go say something to them?"

Before she said anything to me, Mom told her sister about how Mrs. Thomas went to the hospital after an abusive situation with her husband. I also had mentioned that to my auntie Chris when Cassie and I went to lunch with her.

"Hey, Carmen Browne," Michael said in a silly way.

"Hey. So you guys are leaving, huh?" I said as we walked over to them.

My mom sort of hit me. I guess that was none of my business to ask. Learning how to stay in my place was something I was still working on.

My mom went up and hugged Michael's mom. "I've been praying for you, lady," she said to her.

"I'm feeling so much better. I thank you and all of the neighbors for the cards, prayers, and the food. I just thank you guys for everything. It's been hard, but I'm in the process of rebuilding my life. Life's getting better. We're going to move on. I've gotten a job down in Orlando at Disney."

"Oh, that's great," my mother said.

"Yeah, that's really great!" I chimed in.

"Oh, that's only because you think you're going to get some passes," Mike said playfully.

"Michael," I huffed.

Michael laughed and said, "Tell your brother I'll come over to say good-bye to him later."

"My husband is staying in the house until it sells, but the kids and I are leaving today. I want to get them settled before school starts. Mike, don't you have something to say to Carmen?"

He walked up to me without any silliness and said, "When you moved here last year, I gave you a hard time, picking on you and stuff. Now I feel bad about that, and now that I'm about to move to a new place, I want to apologize to you. It's never right to bully anyone. I'm sorry, Carmen."

He held out his hand and I shook it. He didn't have to tell me he was sorry. It was so long ago I really didn't care anymore, but when he said it, it took me back to that time. It did hurt my feelings pretty bad. That's actually how Riana and I became close. She told me he gave most kids a tough time. His words stung, and not just a little. Now hearing him apologize, hearing him say he was sorry and that he wanted to make this right before he left, made me realize that we all need second chances. Being a Christian meant I had to forgive just like God had forgiven me. I didn't know if Mike was one or not, but I believe God was pleased with both of us.

Mike Thomas had taught me something important. Never be too big to set things right.

❂

At nine o'clock, I was in Sunday school class. My teacher Minister Young read from Isaiah 30:21, "And thine ears shall hear a word behind thee, saying, This is the way, walk ye in it, when ye turn to the right hand, and when ye turn to the left." That was our lesson for the day.

God was awesome, showing me Himself more and more. I had prayed for direction, and now He was teaching me things. I was reading a passage that talked about God's guidance. I was smiling from ear to ear.

My teacher noticed and said, "Miss Browne, what's got you all happy this morning?"

I had to giggle as I responded, "I was just talking to God about this yesterday."

"Really now?"

"Yes, sir. I asked Him to lead me to be better and to not be so mean all the time. Now here I am about to have some answers on how to do that. It's cool."

"Wow," Minister Young said. "Don't I wish all of my students would feel that way. That lets me know that my lesson is right on target. Young people, it's not enough just to believe that God is out there. You've got to want Him to order your steps."

"Order them?" someone yelled out.

"Yes," Minister Young replied. "You have to want to walk where He wants you to go, not where you want to go. Kind of like what Carmen just said, but how do you do that? What's a walk with God like? I was thinking about this when I was reading one of my wife's books by one of her favorite authors, Stormie Omartian, *Just Enough Light for the Step I'm On*. It gave me my lesson for today. The title of the book just grabbed my attention."

That's how I felt when I woke up this morning. I didn't know what my walk was going to be like the rest of the day. I just knew how I felt right then. I felt excited in that moment. If that's what walking with God was all about, having Him with you step-by-step, then I felt like I could do this. My attention went back to Minister Young.

He began, "As a parent teaches a baby to walk, eventually the parent wants the child to walk on his own. They want the baby to one day let go of their hands. They want the baby to walk freely by himself."

Yeah, I could relate to that. My parents had video of me taking my first steps. They held me as I walked; then they would let go when it looked like I was walking steady enough to do it on my own.

Minister Young told us it wasn't that way in our walk with Christ. God didn't want us to walk on our own at all. When we accepted Him into our lives, He wanted us to put our hands in His hand, and He would guide our every step.

Minister Young said, "So that's how it is, class, in a nutshell. You take the steps, but you've got to trust that God has got your back, and your front and sides—all of that."

We laughed.

"I'm for real. Walking with God just keeps you thinking about Him and praying to Him like Carmen did. Even if you don't understand, just wait and He will give you the answers you need. Just like the message of my wife's book. God may not show you a path bright with sunshine so that you'll see too far ahead; but you'll have to trust that for middle school, high school, and the rest of your life, He'll take care of you. He just wants you to trust Him for today. Follow Him today and let Him guide you today. You'll see that it's enough light. With that said, here's next week's memory verse, Psalm 119:105. 'Thy word is a lamp unto my feet, and a light unto my path.'"

✪

Three hours later it was the end of church service. Our pastor was making a call to the congregation for people to come to the altar and accept Christ. I looked down the pew at my mom and she smiled at me, knowing that although I had already accepted Him a couple of weeks ago in my sister's bedroom, this public step was one that I needed to take. Now that I had more of an understanding about what walking with God was all about, I was even more excited about going to the altar. Putting my first foot out in the aisle, I stepped on the red carpet and nervously walked the aisle to publicly declare my relationship with Christ.

My pastor bent down and whispered to me, "Miss Browne, you're here to do what this morning, young lady?"

"I'm here to say I've accepted Jesus Christ in my heart and say that I want Him to live with me always."

"All right, you stand right over there. Heaven is rejoicing," he said.

My pastor made a plea for more to come, but nobody else had moved. It was just my day. It was my time to stand for God.

And just as I thought, *I'm the only one here; this is my time; this is my day,* I felt something inside me say that I should want anyone else who wasn't saved to come and stand with me. But if I had to stand alone for God, I would say I believed even if nobody else did, but I didn't want that to be the case.

I bowed my head and prayed aloud beside my pastor, "If there are others, Lord, let them come."

My eyes filled with tears as I saw Clay putting his foot into the aisle, and right behind him was Cassie. The whole church stood up and clapped as my siblings walked down the aisle too. My parents came down the aisle, as well, to support us.

The pastor stood up and talked for a little while longer and the choir sung, "Just a Closer Walk with Thee."

The pastor raised his hands in the air, and then he stood behind me with one hand on my shoulder as he talked. Cassie was on my left and Clay was on my right. My parents stood over to the side, full of pride.

"This is amazing," the pastor spoke. "Three young people from the same household have chosen to give their lives to God. Their parents have been great examples. To have all three come and say to me in their own words why they are here shows they have no doubt that the Lord is real. Isn't it exciting to know the Lord is saving young lives? Changing our young people for Him. Please extend your hands toward this family as we pray."

The rest of the day was just as grand. My family went out to dinner. We had a lot to celebrate. We celebrated the fact that my aunt and her husband were getting back together, and we celebrated Cassie, Clay, and I giving our lives to Christ.

After my dad prayed for the meal, he said, "Having my three children accept Christ is better than any football victory I will ever receive; and, Lord, You know how much those mean to me. Thanks for leading their hearts to You."

We all laughed, but we all knew that my dad was serious. We had made his day, his week, his month, and maybe even his year.

Snake told me that the Christian walk was the best one I could be on. At that moment I knew he was right. As I looked around at my family, I knew I was blessed. I had a lot to work on. I could lose the attitude and not be so prideful. But I was Carmen Browne, a hardhead. But now I knew of the One who could make me better. He was able to soften me for Him.

When we got home, my uncle Mark was waiting in his car. He had gotten there a little early. Cassie and I were a little afraid to say anything to him, but step-by-step, with our parents looking, we walked over to him and he apologized. Seeing him cry made me feel compassion for him. I believed that he really did love my auntie Chris. No one was perfect, but I was hopeful about the way he was trying to make things better for the two of them.

I walked over to Auntie Chris and kissed her on the

cheek as my brother and dad brought out her bags. "You're gonna be okay."

"You're gonna be okay too. And you and Cassie know I'm just a call away if you ever need to talk about anything."

She handed us prisms, and as we turned them a little, they started shining in every direction.

"These are cool," Cassie said.

"What's this for?" I asked.

"A little something special I bought for you girls at the restaurant's gift shop. The reflection sometimes is dull, but when you turn it toward heaven, it sparkles, and all of its sides are beautiful. That's the way it is with your lives now that you've given them to Christ. Sometimes it may appear that your lives are dull, but just keep turning toward Him. Because in Him your lives are always shining, just like this bright beam."

9

Shining Light

It was such a pretty day in August, the day of my so-called birthday party. I had sent out invitations to all of my friends and even told my brother and sister to invite some of their buddies. It was just going to be a backyard barbecue—no clowns, moon-walk or anything extra special. I had out-grown all that. I just wanted to spend time with my friends and celebrate turning eleven.

As my dad took the hamburgers off the grill and went inside, I sat there all alone among the party decorations. It was fifteen minutes into my scheduled party time, 1:15, and no one was there but me. Even Clay and Cassie had decided to do something else with their friends. I guess I was getting what I deserved.

My mom brought different kinds of potato chips to the food table and then sat down with me.

"Birthday girl. Look at the sun shining so bright up there today. You can't be down. I'm not gonna let you be down. School doesn't start for another couple of weeks, you're eleven, and you're gonna be baptized next week. Smile."

"How can I smile, Mom? I'm the party," I sulked and said.

"Sweetheart, your friends will be here soon. It's the summertime. They're coming."

"Clay and Cassie didn't even want to be here. Riana and Layah are probably still mad at me. Mom . . ."

I couldn't even finish the rest of my thoughts. I had disappointed people close to me in the last couple of weeks. Even though I'd asked God for forgiveness, I didn't personally let my friends know that I wanted their forgiveness too.

"So you really think that you're the reason why no one is here, huh? Because you let your friends down?"

"Yes, Mom."

"Well, come with me inside and help me bring out the drinks."

"For what? We're not gonna need them."

"Oh, girl, come on," she said, pulling my hand.

"It's too hot, Mom. I'm sweating. But it's not gonna matter. I'm not gonna have to look cute for a party that I won't be having," I said as we neared the sliding back door. "If I could just get one more chance to say how sorry I am, I would."

"Because they didn't come to your party?" she looked over and asked me.

"No, even though that would have been nice, it's because I feel bad. I don't want to take people for granted. I don't want to be so bossy and have things my way. God is working on me."

"Well, He's working for you too. You go first."

I shrugged my shoulders, unsure of what she was talking about. As soon as I walked inside the dark family room, people jumped out from everywhere and said, *"Surprise!"*

I couldn't believe it. I looked to the left and saw Layah and Riana. Standing on my right was my brother and sister with some of their friends, who were holding presents in their hands. When I looked straight ahead I saw Spence. He was smiling.

I turned around and hugged my mother so tight. "Thank you, Mom. Thank you. You got me good." I'd been outside for about twenty minutes and didn't see any cars come up.

I turned from the embrace and said to everyone, "You guys mean a lot to me. Thanks for coming to my birthday party. True friendships and relationships are built on give-and-take and I've learned that it's not all about Carmen Browne. Thank you, guys, for making my birthday special."

My brother interrupted my sentiments and said, "Let's get this party started!"

Everyone rushed past me into the backyard. Everyone except Layah and Riana.

Riana walked up to me and wiped my tears away. "This is a happy time, girl."

"What? You thought we were gonna miss your party?" Layah said as she slightly socked me on the arm.

"If you would have missed it, I would have deserved it," I said to both of them.

"Yeah, right," Layah said. "None of us are good 100 percent of the time. I was rude when you guys came to my house. It wasn't your fault you guys were late, but I wanted what I wanted; and when I didn't get it, I took it out on y'all. You forgave me and we ended up having a great time. My grandma's even feeling a little better, and I know that's because y'all have been praying. We are friends, Carmen . . . forever."

I looked at the two of them and smiled.

Riana said, "And we're not going anywhere. And next year as middle schoolers, I think we'll be even tighter."

The three of us hugged.

When I went outside, Spence was standing right by the glass door. My friends looked at him and giggled, then told me they would catch up with me in a little while.

"You were waiting on me?" I asked him.

"Yeah, I didn't want to wait until the last minute to speak. I wanted to speak as soon as I got here."

"Spence, I didn't think you'd come since I was such a jerk the last time we talked."

"It's okay. Now I know you wanted to say hi to me, so we're even. I do want us to be friends, good friends, but I'm not a mind reader, so you'll have to cut me some slack. I'm looking forward to getting to know you better in middle school. Here's your birthday present. I hope you like it."

I didn't know what was in the large, shiny, white-wrapped box with the peach bow, but it was really pretty. I told him thanks and we went to join the rest of my twenty guests and played kick ball.

Later that night my brother and sister were helping me clean up. Before we went inside I said, "Guys, um, I remember not wanting to share my day with y'all, but if it weren't for you guys, I wouldn't have had a day like this at all. Some of your friends actually made the party fun."

"We're just glad they bought gifts for you," Clay said. "We told them if they didn't, then they couldn't come. This was your day, Sis."

"Yeah," Cassie said. "The surprise was our idea. We wanted to have one or two friends over, but we're glad that your friends came. We wanted you to think that none of your friends were coming. We gotcha, Carmen!"

Then my sister took off running and I chased after her. The three of us had such a good time that night. We ate what was left of my birthday cake with my parents.

My dad said, "I'm such a blessed man. I have a great family, smart kids who get along with each other, a beautiful wife who is blessed with artistic talent, and I'm looking forward to the football season. I don't know if it will bring winning games or not, but with a family like this to come home to, I've already got everything I need."

He kissed my mom, and the three of us said, "Awww."

Yep. It was a great day. I was blessed.

✪

A week later, I was in Sunday school with my pastor and my brother and sister. Four other people were with us as we had our last session with him to get us ready for our baptism. We learned in the Word that this was a symbol of us giving our lives to Christ. Being immersed in the water was a symbol of pureness, holiness, righteousness, and godliness. Not that we would know how to operate in all of that when we came up out of the water, but the goal was for us to know that we did possess those qualities inside because of the Holy Spirit dwelling within us.

"Do you guys have any questions?" Pastor Wright asked.

Cassie said, "I'm feeling a little nervous about going under the water and all. Is it gonna go up my nose?"

"No, hopefully not, I'm a pro at this whole thing. As long as you don't panic, you should go into the water and come right up with no problem. No need to be scared. Remember why you're doing this," he said.

I chimed in, "For God."

"Correct, Carmen. As long as you know you're doing it for Him and you're asking Him to be with you, then just let the water relax you. You'll feel better than any sprinkler you guys have run through this summer. Lord, I just pray for these young people and Mr. Jackson, who is also ready to give his life to the Lord. Today they are going to be baptized, as another way of showing You how much they love You, Lord. As they embark upon this Christian journey, I just pray that they always follow Your light. May they desire the things You want for them, Lord. I pray You help them forget their past guilt and rid them of anything else that the world attempts to put on them, Father. Help them know that to be Your child, they should strive for godly excellence. May You show them what that is. In Jesus Christ's name we pray. Amen."

We all chimed in, "Amen."

As the church service came to an end about three hours later, my mom was in the ladies' room with Cassie and me, helping us get prepared for the special event. We had to wear all white and we had already put white swimming caps on our heads to protect our hair. Clay went to put on a white T-shirt and white pants. Cassie and I slipped on the white gowns our mom had sewn for us.

She stood beside us and said, "Oh, girls, this is such a big day. You guys are ready to walk with God. I'm so proud of you both. The Holy Spirit will always lead and guide you all." She reached over and hugged us tight.

The next thing I remember, I was standing in the warm water looking up at the shining light. My pastor had one hand behind me and the other was raised toward heaven.

He said, "Upon the confession of your faith, and by all the rights given to me by the Holy Spirit and this great church, I do baptize you, Carmen Lynn Browne, in the name of the Father, the Son, and the Holy Ghost."

He took me backward, and, as I was in the beautiful blue water, the light that I kept looking at shined on me down under.

I prayed silently, Lord, I love You.

As I rose out of the water, it rushed down the front of my face and down my body. That cool feeling was like God saying to me with a big wet kiss, "Carmen, I love you too."

Clay and Cassie went down in the water right after me. They both said that they felt different, like they were showing everyone that they wanted to live for Christ.

I was all smiles when I heard the congregation singing, "Oh, Lord, I just come from the fountain, just from the fountain, Lord, I just come from the fountain; His name is so sweet."

My father was waiting on the other end with the deacons to help us. He handed us towels and said, "You all have always known your daddy's love for you, and now you really know that your heavenly Father loves you too. You're blessed, children. Remember to let His Spirit shine inside you. If you do that, you'll be okay. Your spirit will be like the finest gold. Priceless."

I was thankful that my daddy loved me so. He was right. Now we officially had two fathers. We were special because God sent His Son to die for our sins and make us whole again.

The rest of the day, I celebrated with my family. My dad's parents, Grandpa Harry and Grandma Annabelle, had come and brought my grandma Lula with them. My auntie Chris and uncle Mark didn't come, but I was happy to hear from my grandmother that they were doing fine.

My grandma Annabelle commented on the pretty gold cross that I was wearing. Everyone at the table looked and laughed.

I had to go ahead and tell her that my friend Spence brought over a really big box for my birthday. I opened one box, and inside it was another smaller box. Opened the smaller box and inside of that one was a smaller box. I went on doing that for five boxes until I finally opened the last one and inside of it was a beautiful gold chain with a gold cross on it and a note that said, "I'm glad you're a Christian too."

"Aww, that's so sweet," my family said, laughing.

"I'm gonna have to watch that little Spence," my dad said, "buying my little girl a necklace."

The adults laughed again.

✪

On Monday my mom told Clay, Cassie, and me that she wanted papers about what we had learned this summer on her desk by five o'clock. With school just around the corner, I knew that I needed to practice. I knew with middle school coming up that I had to step up my game and be ready. I had learned a lot this summer, so when she gave us a word count of two hundred words, I stayed in my room all day to prepare my paper.

After dinner my mom walked out onto the patio with three papers in her hand. Clay, Cassie, and I looked at each other and knew what was up. We would have to read them out loud to my father and grandparents.

"Mom," we all whined in different ways simultaneously.

"Oh, come on, guys. They're all good. Public speaking is a skill that takes practice. Who better to practice on than your own family? Cassie, you're up first."

"'What I Learned this Summer'", by Cassie Browne. What I learned this summer is that Jesus loves me. I used to just know it from a song that I learned when I was a baby called, 'Yes, Jesus Love Me.' Now I know it because I feel it in my heart. I am always able to talk to Him anytime I want. When I'm feeling sad, I think about all that He has given me—a mommy and a daddy that love me,

grandparents who care, and even a brother and a sister who I like most of the time. Even when we have sad times in our lives, like this summer when I was hurt at Auntie Chris and Uncle Mark's house, we know that God is there. I learned that we have to listen to each other and not let our tempers make us say mean things. Thinking about my family lets me know that God loves me. I was just baptized, but now I feel different. I believe that God will help me be a better little girl. I pray that everyone loves Jesus and lets Him into their hearts. The end," my sister concluded by doing a curtsey bow.

We all clapped. It was special to know that both she and I felt the same way about God. He loves us and we were happy we knew it.

"All right, Clay, you're up, Son," my mom said.

My brother got up and dragged his feet and took the paper from my mom and cleared his throat.

"This summer I learned not to be so into me, but to follow Jesus Christ. I was blessed to see that life isn't all about everything Clay Browne wants. I learned to trust God in everything He gives. At one point, I wanted a different family, but He showed me that I've got the best family there is. A dad who encourages me to excel not only in sports but also in all that I do. I want to make him proud of me. God has given me a mother who, though sometimes I feel that I'm too big for certain things that she does for

me, I know it makes her happy to do those things for me, and I feel loved because of it. I'm blessed because I have two sisters whom I sometimes love to bother, but now I want to protect them too. I want to make life better for them. Again, I learned this summer not to be so into me."

My dad stood up and hugged my brother. It was a cool moment. The three of us had learned so much this summer. We were so blessed. We had a great family who wasn't perfect but was strong. Not strong in our own might but strong believers in Jesus Christ. Knowing that made me excited about middle school, high school, college, whatever future God wanted for me. Now I knew that I wasn't just here for this world, but I was getting ready for heaven.

"Well, last, we have Miss Carmen Browne, my oldest daughter who just had a birthday. Carmen, honey, it's your turn."

I was all nervous about reading my paper, but the confidence I had just felt listening to my brother let me know that I could do it. Being a little nervous was okay, but I needed to trust that God was going to read every word with me. He was going to stand with me, be with me, and give me the strength I needed.

I began, *"This summer I accepted Jesus Christ as my Savior and I am grateful for all that the Holy Spirit has taught me through God's Word, my family, and other*

Christians. I learned that I could talk to God anywhere about anything. He is my Father and cares about His children just like a natural father. I don't have to be perfect, but I should trust God to take care of every need that I have.

"I also witnessed domestic violence. I learned that domestic violence can be verbally threatening or physically harming someone in the family. This time it wasn't just something I had seen on TV or read in a book, but I experienced it firsthand. Because I want my way sometimes, I know dealing with people can be tough. When one person wants their way and doesn't want to compromise, the way they try to control the situation can be displeasing to God and hurtful to others. I learned that when one person is being emotionally or physically abused, they should seek help. In some situations the police can be called to rescue someone, or a pastor can work with people who want to be counseled, and a hotline can be contacted for confidential counseling. The important thing is to let a trusted person know what's going on. No matter what we do, we should pray for the people involved in the situation. All of us need to calm down and listen to people we love even when we don't agree with them, and control our tempers. We can do that with the help of the Lord. I hope more people learn about this problem so that the world can be rid of it altogether, but until then, I will pray that God helps the world to communicate better. We can help people affected by domestic violence if we follow God's shining light."

The Negro National Anthem

Lift every voice and sing
Till earth and heaven ring,
Ring with the harmonies of Liberty;
Let our rejoicing rise
High as the listening skies,
Let it resound loud as the rolling sea.
Sing a song full of the faith that the dark past has taught us,
Sing a song full of the hope that the present has brought us,
Facing the rising sun of our new day begun
Let us march on till victory is won.

So begins the Black National Anthem, written by James Weldon Johnson in 1900. Lift Every Voice is the name of the joint imprint of The Institute for Black Family Development and Moody Publishers.

Our vision is to advance the cause of Christ through publishing African-American Christians who educate, edify, and disciple Christians in the church community through quality books written for African Americans.

Since 1988, The Institute for Black Family Development, a 501(c)(3) non-profit Christian organization, has been providing training and technical assistance for churches and Christian organizations. The Institute for Black Family Development's goal is to become a premier trainer in leadership development, management, and strategic planning for pastors, ministers, volunteers, executives, and key staff members of churches and Christian organizations. To learn more about The Institute for Black Family Development, write us at:

15151 Faust
Detroit, Michigan 48223

We hope you enjoy this book from Moody Publishers. Our goal is to provide high-quality, thought-provoking books and products that connect truth to your real needs and challenges. For more information on other books and products written and produced from a biblical perspective, go to www.moodypublishers.com or write to:

Moody Publishers
820 N. LaSalle Boulevard
Chicago, IL 60610

The author would love to hear from you.

To contact

Stephanie Perry Moore

E-mail her at

dsssmoore@aol.com